AWAKENED

SHADOW GUILD: HADES & PERSEPHONE BOOK 2

LINSEY HALL

For Helen, who is so smart, kind, and beautiful that I'm pretty sure she stepped out of the pages of a book.

1

Seraphia

When one walks into hell, it's important to be prepared.

Too bad I could hardly stand.

"How are you doing?" Mac, one of my closest friends, asked from my side. She supported me around the waist, and it was her lean strength I had to thank for getting me this far.

"Fine. Doing great." My insides felt like they'd been put through a blender.

"You look great," Mac said. "The deathly pallor and hollow eyes really suit you."

I huffed a weak laugh and stared at the door of the Guild City library, fear yawning wide inside me. It created a chasm as deep and dark as Hades' heart.

It was time to go back to hell.

"You're sure about this?" Mac asked.

I looked at her, grateful for the faint rain on my face. It was a dreary day in Guild City, but the cool rain was soothing against the heat that flickered through me from the pomegranate potion.

Curse, more like.

"Do I look like I have any other options?" I asked.

"No." Anger twisted her pretty features. "I just hate this for you. It's all my fault."

"Shut up, or I swear to God, I'll kick you in the tits."

She huffed a laugh. "You couldn't manage that on your best day."

She wasn't wrong. I was far too short, and she was far too quick and tough. Being a librarian gave me a certain set of skills, but definitely not tit-kicking.

I turned back to the library door, staring at the dark wood and tiny panes of glass.

This is it.

I was walking back into the underworld, compelled by Hades himself. It'd been two weeks since I'd escaped, and the pomegranate potion he'd given me was forcing me to return. It was about to kill me, which was the only thing worse than seeing Hades again.

Lie.

Part of me wanted to see him. But I shoved that part back, bound it with duct tape, and shoved it in a closet. A bit serial-killery of me, but effective.

I drew in a deep breath and stared at the door of the library. It was the portal to hell, which I definitely hadn't known when I'd taken the job. But I'd be going back prepared this time.

Last time, I'd been hampered by my need to find Mac a cure for another of Hades' curses. This time, it was just me, trying to find a way to break the pomegranate curse. I'd tried everything I could here on earth, searching high and low. My potion master friend Eve had done everything she could as well, but without the pomegranate that had cursed me, her hands had been tied.

"I'm here!" A voice sounded from down the street, and I turned to look.

As if she'd heard me thinking about her, Eve raced toward me down the uneven, cobblestone street. Her purple hair streamed in the wind, and she raised two big leather bags, a smile stretched across her pretty Fae face. She skidded to a stop in front of me. "Got all kinds of potions for you here. Hades won't know what hit him."

"Thank you." I smiled gratefully but didn't bother to take the bags. No way I could lift something so heavy in my state. "I can never pay you back for this. Your help will save me."

"Psh, don't worry about that." She frowned at me, looking me up and down. "You're going back not a moment too soon."

"Don't I know it." At the words, pain stabbed my

insides. I gasped and doubled over, clutching my belly. It felt like my organs were trying to leap out of my body and run right back to hell.

"Let's go," Mac said. "With any luck, you'll feel better once you're there."

"Except for the fact that I'll be stuck in hell."

Mac nodded. "Except for that."

"Onward." I straightened my shoulders, reminding myself that I was going armed. Come hell or high water, I'd make Hades regret dosing me with the pomegranate potion.

Mac pushed open the old wooden door and stepped forward. I resisted briefly, turning to look at Guild City. I *would* be coming back. I wouldn't settle for any less.

But all the same, I wanted one last peek at my home.

The quiet streets of Guild City looked like something right out of Shakespeare. It was pure Tudor, the dark timber buildings coated in white plaster. Hundreds of mullioned windows watched me like silent eyes.

The people who filled the streets were modern, and several drove motorbikes down the narrow lanes. The wares in the shop windows were a combination of magical and mundane. Each display danced colorfully behind the glass, magic making the objects move in order to entice customers. I drew in a deep breath and turned back to the library.

Mac and Eve helped me through the door, each supporting me with a shoulder under my arm. Every step was agony as we entered the hallowed halls of my gorgeous library. The gleaming tile floors echoed underfoot, and the domed ceiling soared overhead. Magical candles flared to life, illuminating the tall wooden shelves and millions of leather-bound volumes.

I breathed deeply of the paper and oak–scented air, letting it fill my lungs with the scent of home. I'd hardly spent any time here since my escape from Hades. No one else had been allowed in, either, just in case he planned to grab someone as leverage.

Now, I was headed right for his portal.

Right for him.

"Nearly there," Mac said.

I nodded weakly, forcing one aching foot in front of the other. I'd never been in such pain in all my life, and I had Hades to thank for it. I'd resisted returning for as long as I could, but at this point, I'd honestly rather be dead. Slowly, we crossed the floor underneath the great dome, heading deeper into the stacks.

"I'm going to stash these bags in the ether," Eve said. "The spell is connected to you, so you'll be able to retrieve them anywhere."

I looked at her, gratitude welling within me. She was the premier potion maker in Guild City, and she'd kitted me out with thousands of pounds' worth of potions. Mac had contributed weapons, and my friend Carrow's familiar—a raccoon named Cordelia—had found me the best snacks in Carrow's cupboard. I could probably eat of the underworld now that I'd taken the pomegranate potion, but I couldn't be too careful.

"I just wish you'd let me go with you," Mac said.

"Hell, no. Not until I know it's safe." I shook my head hard, nearly going blind as pain exploded behind my eyes. "Bollocks, that hurts."

Mac tightened her arm around my waist to keep me up. "You'll feel right as rain in no time."

"And ready to murder Hades," I muttered, rage warming me from within. I was going to kill that bastard for doing this to me. Whatever semi-soft feelings I'd developed for him were long gone after what I'd been through.

We reached the stacks at the back of the library. A dark mist began to rise up from the ground, smelling of firelight and ash.

Hades.

"He knows we're here." I pulled away from my friends, nearly going to my knees. "You need to go."

"Take this." Eve thrust a tiny vial at me, then retreated from the mist. "Invisibility potion. It won't last long, but it will give you time to get your bearings before he sees you."

"Thank you." Invisibility potions were exceedingly rare. I gulped it down, feeling the chill of the magic as it raced over my skin. Mac and Eve blinked at me, their gazes suddenly searching.

"It worked," Eve said.

All around, the mist began to rise higher. Eve and Mac watched it warily, stepping backward as it curled toward them. Breathing too much of it would land them in a hell of a lot of trouble, as Mac had learned three weeks ago.

"Get out of here," I said. "I'll be fine."

"Wish I'd hugged you," Mac said.

"Same."

She smiled.

"I'll hug you when I get back," I said. "Now go!"

The mist had reached my knees and continued to crawl toward them.

"Be safe," Eve said.

"Of course."

Mac and Eve gave me—or rather, the place where they'd last seen me—one last look, then turned and fled. I sucked in a deep breath and spun back to the mist. It rose quickly, prickling against my limbs. It should have felt horrible.

Instead, it felt like a caress.

I drew in a shuddery breath, hating what it could make me feel.

"I'm coming for you, you bastard." I set my jaw and staggered farther into the mist. I only made it a few feet before going to my knees, the pain too much to bear. Rage flared in my chest.

He'd done this to me.

Hand over hand, I crawled toward the deepest part

of the mist, a jet-black pool that must be the origin. The portal. He'd be here at any moment, and I didn't want him setting foot in my precious library.

Tears of frustration and pain stung my eyes as my arms gave out. Every limb felt like it was being eaten by acid from the inside, and it seemed as if I were breathing through water.

I'm dying.

There was no question—I'd waited until the very last moment to return to Hades, and this was the result.

Bastard.

I pushed myself farther, army crawling across the cold tile floor, my vision nearly gone from weakness.

Finally, I reached the black pool. I could hear the sound of his magic—waves crashing against a cliff wall —and taste it on my tongue—dark, bitter chocolate. I dragged myself into the deepest, darkest part of his magic, feeling it all around me, suffocating. It grabbed hold of me, dragging me through the ether and spinning me through space.

For one blissful, exhilarating second, I felt nothing, just the wild spin of the ether as it took me to hell.

Then I collapsed on the cold ground of another library.

Panting, I lay on the stone floor, staring up at the ceiling that soared overhead. In a split second, I took it all in. Ah, yes. I was back in the library that Halloween forgot.

The stone rafters had been carved from an ebony rock. Narrow and arching, they looked like bones blackened by fire. On either side of me, oak bookshelves soared tall, filled to the brim with tomes bound in dark leather. Spiderwebs stretched in front of the volumes, glittering like string threaded with diamonds. Emerald and amethyst spiders skittered across the webs, beautiful yet terrifying.

And yet, every bone wasn't aching. My muscles didn't feel like shredded meat. Even my lungs worked properly.

I'm better.

The physical effects of the potion had worn off. Relief surged through me, and a massive grin spread across my face.

Oh, thank fates.

Only seconds had passed since I'd arrived, but Hades....

Was he here?

I sat up, keeping my movements and my breathing silent. With any luck, my invisibility potion should be holding strong.

The door to the library burst open, slamming against the wall. Hades strode in, power incarnate, lethal and terrifyingly beautiful—that is, if *beautiful* commanded an army of the dead and personally tortured the shit out of the fallen souls in his realm.

His ocean-dark gaze searched the library for any

sight of me, his strong jaw set with determination. The sight of him standing in the door, dark cape flowing back from his broad shoulders and his body cast in shadow, sent me back to the moment I'd escaped this place.

I'd nearly made it to the portal when he'd blasted through the door, shirtless and glorious, with his golden wings flared wide and his body corded with muscles hewn in war. Rage had vibrated from every atom of him, his fallen angel's face terrible in his anger and grief.

His beauty made me hate him all the more.

"Seraphia." His voice rumbled like thunder, deep and low, flowing inside me like smoke and filling me up with a prickling tension. "I know you're here."

Silently, I rose. I stood only fifty feet from him, right in plain sight. Thank fates for Eve's potion, which was definitely working.

Silently, I stepped to the side, creeping toward a bookshelf. He just needed to get farther into the library and leave the door open. Then, I could sneak around him and get the hell out of here. With any luck, I might be able to find the cure for the pomegranate potion without ever speaking to him at all. Then I could escape forever and never see him again.

It'd take all the luck in the world for my plan to work out that way, and I was ridiculously short on the stuff.

Still, I'd try

He strode deeper into the library. There was no

sunlight in this miserable place, but he stepped into a pool of light cast by the chandelier above. The sight of him nearly made me gasp.

He looked like hell.

His cheekbones were even sharper, his ocean eyes shadowed like the grave. Once again, he was dressed entirely in black leather armor, down to his gloves. His shoulders were just as broad, but I had a feeling I'd find the muscles cut even more fiercely. Hewn like iron. There was something raw about him, as if he'd been pared down to his basest parts.

Is this what my absence had done to him?

I swallowed hard, having no idea what to make of it.

Get it together, ninny.

I crept toward the door, determined to ignore the tortured twist of his lips as he looked around the library, clearly searching for me. Silently, I slipped by him, holding my breath so that I made no sound at all. Fortunately, my trainers were silent on the tile floor, my jeans and loose jumper easy to move in.

A second later, I slipped out the door and into the underworld. From where I stood at the top of the library steps, it sprawled out in front of me. It was midday here, the sky a murky gray. The sun never shone. I still didn't know if there even *was* a sun.

Once again, I was struck by how his home was a dark shadow of my own. Like Guild City, a massive wall surrounded the town, but this city was built on top of a mountain. On the other side of the circular wall, the world fell away, becoming flat plains, forests, oceans, and lakes.

Yet all of it was so dark. So devoid of life.

It didn't stop it from being incredible.

From here, it felt like I stood on top of the world. The library was higher than everything else in the city except the castle at the other end of the avenue that cut through the town.

The buildings were ornate structures of black stone and glass. The stone itself was carved in swoops and swirls, while the glass gleamed like water. If I could lose myself amongst those buildings, it would buy me even more time.

I couldn't help but peek back over my shoulder, spotting Hades still standing in the middle of the library.

He was perfectly still, head bowed, dark hair flowing longer than it had been last time. His broad shoulders curved inward slightly, and his hands clenched at his sides.

Did he think it was a false alarm?

Was it disappointment I saw on him?

No way. And even if it was, it wasn't like he was disappointed not to see me. Whatever we'd shared had been about him trying to use me for his own purposes, not because he cared about me.

I turned and ran, sprinting silently down the stairs

toward the main street. Thank fates Eve had stashed the bags in the ether. I'd never be this quick or quiet if I had to carry them myself.

As I ran, I couldn't help but delight in the strength of my body, my swiftness. I'd never considered myself exceptionally quick or strong, but after the pomegranate curse, it felt amazing.

Fortunately, the night wolves were nowhere to be seen. The Children of Cerberus would definitely be able to smell me, and I didn't need their attention, even though I was fairly certain they wouldn't hurt me.

A few moments later, I reached the street and darted toward the back alleys. I'd never been anywhere but the main avenue that stretched between the library and his fortress, but I didn't want to be out in the open when the potion wore off.

The alley was dark and narrow, but thankfully, empty. I hurried deeper into the city, finding a quiet little alcove to hide in. I pressed myself into it and leaned against the wall, panting.

I'd been planning this for days, but my mind had been so fogged by pain that it had been hard to come up with a concrete scheme. I had *no* idea how to get a cure, but maybe the apothecary would know. Not only did she have the skills, but she was my only ally in this whole place.

If I could just get to her cottage behind the castle, I'd have a chance.

I slipped away from the alcove and made my way through the city. As I cut through the narrow streets and alleys, I didn't see anyone. It was difficult to determine the correct direction, but occasionally, I glimpsed the castle towers above the roof lines of the houses.

I'd only gone a short way when a tiny black bat swooped down in front of me.

"Echo!" I whispered, delighted.

The tiny bat had become my friend last time I'd been here. Maybe even my familiar. He'd certainly been a huge help.

From up ahead, he spun around and fluttered back toward me, his tiny face as cute as a mouse's. He landed on my shoulder for the briefest second, and it felt like a hug. Warmth flared through me.

"Can you lead me to the castle?" I whispered. "The quickest way."

Echo launched himself off my shoulder and fluttered down the street. I ran to catch up, trying to keep my breathing quiet as it grew ragged.

The little bat swooped around turns and flew low to the ground. Soon, we'd reached the fortress. I pressed myself against a building wall and looked up at the enormous structure. It was a terrifying, hulking thing, yet strangely beautiful.

Just like Hades.

And I was here to face him.

I stepped forward, grateful that I still seemed to be

invisible. There were a few people out and about, but they paid me no heed. As I stepped toward the castle, I felt seething strange. Like magic in the air.

My magic.

And it was coming from the back of the castle.

What the hell?

2

Seraphia

My heart pounded as I hurried toward the fortress and climbed the stairs, sticking to the shadows despite the fact that I was probably still invisible. Thankfully, it was possible to sneak around the side wall toward the back. Hades had a minimal number of guards on the whole place because he simply wasn't worried about anyone defying him. He *owned* hell.

No one would dare challenge him here.

Except me.

I was going to get the cure for this pomegranate potion so that I could get the hell out of here. But along the way, I'd teach him not to screw with me. I'd been the mild-mannered librarian my whole life, and that was *over.*

Quietly, I sneaked around the side of the massive castle. The stone wall towered to my left, its blocks each the size of a car. The apothecary's cottage sat at the back, along with the strangest sensation of my magic. It was so weird, but it felt like I'd left part of myself back there. It called to me, like my soul was reaching out and wanting to be reconnected—except I had no idea what that meant.

Finally, I reached the back garden where the apothecary's cottage was located.

Shocked, I stumbled to a halt.

The garden was no longer full of the withered stone plants that had filled it. Instead, massive green vines crawled over the entire place like giant green snakes, glimmering with an emerald brilliance that was nearly blinding.

"Holy fates," I breathed, shocked.

Before I'd left, I'd planted several tiny cuttings, using my magic to give them a little jumpstart toward growth. But this...I'd never expected anything like it.

Awed, I walked deeper into the garden, following a path toward the apothecary's cottage. Normally, I'd be able to see it by now, but the vines grew up in front of it, twisting around each other to form a huge wall. Near the middle of the garden, I spun in a circle.

I'd done this?

It couldn't be possible.

Near me, one of the vines shifted, unfurling from the pile. It reached toward me, a dark ruby flower at the tip. The petals were huge, the bloom the size of my head. It hovered near my shoulder, and as I reached out to touch it, the petals furled back to reveal fangs. I gasped. With the scarlet petals and white fangs, it was terrifying and gorgeous all at once. It stroked my shoulder, and magic pulsed low in my belly.

Dark.

I drew in an unsteady breath.

The magic felt entirely different than it had back on earth. There was a yawning hunger, as if my magic were greedy for power and strength.

This place changes me.

I swallowed hard. My magic felt stronger here, but it also felt darker. These plants were proof of that.

"You left quite a mark," the apothecary's voice sounded from behind me.

I spun to face her. She grinned at me, her long black hair piled in a high ponytail over her head. The pretty starburst tattoo near her eye gleamed.

"You can see me?" I asked.

She nodded. "Invisibility potion?"

"Yeah. Must have worn off." I gestured to the plants around me. "When did this happen?"

"Shortly after you left. They're a bit crazy. Kinda mean." As if to prove her statement, one of the plants struck out at her, the crimson petals pulled back in a snarl and the fangs snapping. She whacked it on the side of the bloom hard enough to make it lose a few petals. "No biting!"

The plant hissed, then pulled back.

She grinned. "They've learned to respect me."

"I just...can't believe this." I was clearly a disaster with my magic, if I'd let something like this happen. How could I possibly be Persephone? The idea of it was ridiculous, given the evidence, so I shoved it to the back of my mind. First things first: a cure for the pomegranate curse.

"I need your help," I said.

"Don't you always?"

It was true. I definitely was going to owe her one. "Yeah, but it's important. It's—"

A faint prickling rose on the air, bringing with it the scent of firelight and the taste of dark chocolate. My eyes widened. "He's coming. Go."

She couldn't be caught with me. It was too dangerous.

The apothecary was no dummy, though. She'd already spun around and disappeared into the vines. I drew in a breath and whirled around to face the direction from which Hades would come.

Did I have time to run?

Nope.

And I didn't want to. I wanted to face him down.

A moment later, he stepped through the vines and into view, his gaze on me. The deep blue of his eyes burned as he took me in, his fists clenching, the thin leather of his gloves gleaming dully in the light.

His magic rolled out from him, so powerful that I nearly staggered. The sound of waves crashing on cliffs was nearly deafening, and the scent of firelight nearly suffocating. He was strength and power personified. A *god*.

It had never been more obvious than now that I was up against the near impossible.

Worse, he looked so damned good that I wanted to kick him.

"You're back," he said. Then the bastard smiled.

He *smiled*.

The memory of the agony I'd suffered, of the choice he'd taken away, flared through me. Rage like I'd never known lit a fire in my chest. It blazed, an inferno that devoured every rational thought in my head.

"You," I hissed.

"Don't pretend you didn't miss this place." His voice rolled like low, distant thunder. "That you didn't miss the darkness."

I hated that he was almost right. That my dreams had sometimes brought me visions of him. Visions of us. And this place made my magic so much more powerful. I could accomplish anything here—I felt the power seething through my veins, wanting to be used. I shrieked, the rage bubbling up until it came out of my mouth as a banshee's wail.

All around, the vines rose up, towering over us like massive snakes. They'd revealed the pomegranate tree in the middle of the garden.

That tree.

I reached for it and clenched a fist. The enormous vines responded, stretching toward the tree and yanking it out of the ground, roots and all.

The most incredible sensation rushed through me— strength and power and confidence. It filled me up like a balm, washing away all my doubts and insecurities and pain.

All I felt was *power.* Pure, unadulterated power.

Hunger for more followed on its heels, along with the rage.

"Stop!" Hades shouted.

"No!" The vines followed my every command, acting before I could consciously form the thought. They tore the tree apart, rending it limb from limb, trunk from roots.

The sheer violence of it, the power, made my blood sing and my mind fog.

This is amazing.

I'd never felt so good in my entire life. The world was chaos around me, but I was calm. The rage had faded, and I was in control.

Hades stared at me from thirty feet away, his gaze

burning into me. Something like triumph flickered in his eyes, but I was too far gone to figure out why.

"Seraphia, stop." A masculine voice sounded from my side, and a hand gripped my arm.

Shock punched me, and I lashed out with the vines, grabbing up the intruder before I'd even turned to look at him. By the time I saw that it was Lucifer, he was already captured by two thick vines wrapping around his chest and thighs.

Yes. Squeeze him.

The thought seemed to come from nowhere, but the vines obeyed. They constricted tighter around the handsome fallen angel who had once been—almost—a friend to me.

Dark delight flared inside me as I watched the frown crease his brow. As his skin flushed darker, the delight only increased.

"Stop!" Hades roared, striding toward me.

Lucifer snarled at me, his power flaring. It smelled of cold rain and sounded like thunder. Massive black wings burst from his back, tearing the vines apart.

Pain shot through me, and I shrieked, stumbling backward.

Freed, Lucifer dropped to the ground, and his wings disappeared. The torn remains of the vines lay scattered all around him, seeping an emerald, viscous fluid that felt like my own blood leaking from my limbs. The pain sharpened my mind, and I gasped.

What the hell was happening to me?

I'd just tried to kill Lucifer.

I would never do a thing like that...yet I had.

I looked for him, but he was already gone, disappeared into the garden.

Panicked, I spun back to face Hades. He was striding toward me, so close that I could see the dark pupils of his eyes and the too-thick lashes that framed them.

A growl rose in his throat as he reached me, his face set in lines of frustration. Without a word, he heaved me into the air and flung me over his shoulder

I shrieked, pounding and kicking his back. "Let me go, you bastard!"

All around, my vines waved in the air—responding to my distress, no doubt, because I certainly wasn't controlling them. I wanted to. I wanted to use them to grab Hades and toss him into the air.

But I couldn't. Not after the way I'd just lost control.

Still, the vines seethed around us, a threatening dance of death that made a shudder run down my spine.

A low growl sounded from Hades' throat. He had one arm wrapped over the back of my thighs like an iron bar, but he lifted the other. It was impossible to see from my position flung over his shoulder, but I could just imagine him with his arm outstretched toward the plants, his hand wrapped in thin black leather. The plants would obey him, even though they were mine. He could control objects with his mind, and they would be no different.

He'd done the same when he'd commanded the night wolves and when he'd forced boulders aside to save our lives at the Temple of Shadows.

All around, the vines began to drop, docile and calm as they curled up on the ground.

"Stop controlling my plants." I tried punching him in the kidneys—or at least, where I thought the kidneys were. He didn't so much as budge.

"You certainly can't be trusted with them," he rumbled.

Well, that was true. But still, I didn't like him controlling what was mine.

"Put me down," I demanded.

"I have no idea why you think I would ever listen to you."

"I'm going to get you for this, you bastard."

"No, you aren't." He turned and strode back toward the castle.

"You have no idea what I'm capable of."

"You're right. I don't. But you're still a fledgling god and no match for me."

I hissed, so angry that I couldn't get so much as a word out.

His long strides ate up the ground, and my stomach bounced painfully against his huge shoulder, reminding me of all I'd suffered the last two weeks. I punched him again, getting nothing but sore knuckles in return.

He stopped at the back door to the castle, and I gave the garden one last look. The sight of the massive, coiled vines sent a shiver down my spine.

I'd nearly killed Lucifer with those vines.

What the hell was wrong with me?

Hades yanked open the castle door and strode inside. He took a convoluted route through the castle, making so many turns that I lost track. Every step made me angrier, and by the time we reached another door, I was a seething mess of rage once again.

He swung open a door and set me on the ground, then stepped back. With horror, I realized that I stood in a dungeon.

A dungeon.

3

HADES

Seraphia stood in front of me, so beautiful that it hurt to look at her. Humans described looking at the setting sun to be painful yet glorious, an agony worth suffering for a glimpse at incredible beauty.

It had to be like staring at Seraphia.

It wasn't just the alignment of her features or the glow of her skin, the sweep of her hair or the curve of her form. It was something that shone within her, and I couldn't identify it.

The memory of her pressed against me burned, an inferno that had imprinted itself against my flesh. I wanted to shake the feeling away, peel the skin off if I needed to.

It weakened me, this insane obsession.

She crossed her arms and glared. "This isn't my room."

I raised a brow, resisting looking away from her. "You forfeited that room when you ran away."

"Of course I ran away, you bastard."

"Well, there will be no running now." I stepped back, needing the space from her, and reached for the door handle. "Unlike last time, this door has a lock."

"A lock?" Shock echoed in her voice.

"I've neither the time nor the desire to chase you." *Lie.* I had the desire to chase her across worlds, and I hated it. "Therefore, you will remain locked in this room until we come to an agreement."

She huffed out a breath, staring at me with such fiery anger that it lit something inside me as well. Her scent wrapped around me, floral and fresh, reminiscent of things I'd never seen. Never cared to see.

Until her.

"Don't look so pleased," she said. "Just because your little plan to drag me back here worked."

"Pleased? You put a hole in my stomach when you left."

"I didn't leave. I escaped. And you were collateral damage. Which I'm fine with, by the way."

That might hurt if I knew how to feel pain. "But you're back now."

"Because you forced me. How long is this damned potion going to stay in my system?"

"Forever."

Anger flashed on her face, but no surprise. She expected me to play dirty. She had no idea.

"I want you to remove it."

"I can't. There's no cure that I know of." It was true, and from the way her face fell, she believed me. Good. She'd stop trying to run. "When I touched you, I could feel the magic going wild inside you. The darkness rising. You liked it."

"I did not."

Pleasure flashed through me. "Then you don't deny that it is there?"

She scowled.

"Let me help you," I said. "I can teach you to master that power. Grow stronger."

She shook her head. "I want nothing to do with it."

"You're a menace to yourself and others if you don't train with it. You could have killed Lucifer."

Guilt flashed in her eyes, then cunning. Her gaze traveled over me, taking in all the details of my attire as the cogs in her mind spun.

She was plotting my downfall, it was certain.

I couldn't blame her. It was what I would do if I were in her position.

The chess game was back on.

"I want nothing to do with you," she said.

It was expected, but still...frustrating.

My hands tingled, and I resisted a frown. I couldn't help clenching my fists inside my leather gloves, though. If I removed them, I knew that I'd see them fading. I'd see *myself* fading.

She wasn't the only one who was cursed. My own curse was acting up as well. I needed to get out of here.

"I'll give you time to think." Before she could say anything, I shut the door in her face and locked it, tucking the key away in my pocked.

"Hades!" Her voice echoed through the door, followed by her pounding fists.

A wry smile tugged at one corner of my mouth, and I strode away, rubbing a hand over my face.

The halls were empty as I strode through them, headed for the pit of darkness at the base of the castle. Now, more than ever, I needed its guidance. Seraphia had the ability to derail me from my task. She hadn't managed it yet, but only an imbecile would underestimate his foe.

I would never underestimate Seraphia.

Not again.

She'd proved herself a more than worthy opponent. Smart and strong, cunning and dangerous—it drew me to her like a moth to flame. The memory of her body pressed against mine flared through me, igniting a desire that was far too human.

I wanted her.

Before she'd come, I hadn't even understood the concept.

I shook the thought away as I reached the stairs that led to the depths of my castle, which were far more austere than the public spaces above. I felt more at home here. It made sense, given that I was the closest thing to a creature built of cold granite.

Quickly, I took the stairs two at a time, descending to the cool, calm darkness that soothed my soul. When I'd touched her, I'd felt darkness, rising and strong. But more than that, I'd felt light. I'd felt the goodness of her soul, her selflessness and willingness to help others. Kindness and generosity.

All so unfamiliar. So foreign.

And yet, so Seraphia.

It unbalanced me.

The air grew cooler as I descended the wide spiral stairwell, the dark magic soothing me.

I stepped out into the large chamber and its almost deafening silence. Unlike the castle above, which had been built by an army of the dead, dark magic had hewn the cavern straight from the rock. Before I'd been born —created, more like—it had crept out of the pit in the center of the room, forming this temple to darkness and power, greed and despair.

I strode toward the pit, my soul quieting as I approached the deep, dark chasm. At the edge, I stared down into the abyss. Gleaming stars swirled in the depths. Whether they were real or a trick of the mind, I had no idea.

As always, the pit called to me. To enter was death—a return to Tartarus, where I would be tortured for what felt like an eternity. Chronos was there, though I had never met him. He was a Titan, and the miserable bastard had been imprisoned there long ago.

It was said that he might be my father—that I was a creation of his magic. The product of his bond with the darkness that imprisoned him in Tartarus. Why I was forced to return every millennium, once my body had fully faded away, I had no idea. But it was as reliable as the setting of the sun.

Memories of that pain filled my mind—endless years of torment in the flames and freezing wind of the worst part of hell. Feeling like my body was liquefied by fire and reformed by ice. It was nothing compared to the punishments I dispensed to the murderers and rapists here in the underworld.

I pulled off the gloves that covered my hands, revealing them to be as I'd expected—partially transparent.

"Damn it." I drew in a steadying breath as I clenched my fists, drawing strength from the dark magic that wafted up from the pit. It flowed over me, filling my soul, re-solidifying my form. For a while, at least.

Time was running out.

This place was both my savior and my despair. It had

formed me, death incarnate, with one purpose: to spread the darkness. I'd been trying for millennia, but without Seraphia, it had been impossible.

Now that I had her, I would succeed, defying my fate and breaking the cycle that dragged me back to Tartarus to be tortured.

I drew in a deep breath, letting the magic of this place soothe the riot in my soul. It forced away the light with which Seraphia had infected me, calming the torment within me. Emotion seeped away, replaced with the calm, cold detachment that kept me sane.

I stared down into the abyss. "She is back."

Good. The voice rumbled through the room, filling the air until it was nearly suffocating. *You will need her to help you find the location and time of doomsday.*

Seraphia

The door slammed in my face, concealing Hades and leaving me alone in the dungeon.

That bastard.

I stared at the solid wooden door, anger surging through me. It tugged at the darkness in my soul that had ignited when I'd arrived here. The anger and rage were so hard to ignore—unnaturally so.

I strode to the door and pulled on it. As expected, it didn't budge. I wanted to kick the damned thing, but that would get me nowhere.

You're a menace to yourself and others. His words echoed in my head.

He was right.

I had more than just the pomegranate problem. *I* was a problem. What had happened with Lucifer...

I liked the guy. I'd never want to hurt him like that. And yet, I had. Worse, I'd *enjoyed* it.

The power had coursed through me on a tidal wave of pleasure, pushing me farther and farther. Being back here made it harder to resist. Being around *Hades* made it harder to resist. When he'd touched me, I'd felt that darkness flare.

I drew in a shuddery breath and shook my head. "Nope. Not going there."

I called upon the ether, trying to remove one of the bags that Eve had given me. It'd be chock full of helpful potions, including something to break through this lock.

But nothing happened. The ether didn't respond.

Damn it. Something was wrong.

This time, I really *did* kick the door, yelping when pain flared.

Aching, knowing I'd been an idiot, I tried to reach into the ether one more time. The spell should be working. It should spit that bag right back out at me.

Yet it didn't.

Either this prison blocked the magic or the underworld itself did.

Fat lot of good all that preparing had done me.

What about the key?

Frantic, I thrust my hand into the pocket of my jeans, finding the key to the library safe within. I sagged, grateful. If that had disappeared somehow, I'd be screwed. I needed it to get back through the library to return home. Unless he'd changed the locks...

Fear iced my spine, but I pushed it away and turned to face the rest of the small dungeon, searching for anything to help me break out. There was nothing but a cot and a bucket.

A bucket?

Holy fates, I was going to kill Hades for this.

My gaze caught on the tiny window set high in the wall. The sky blazed orange as it transitioned to night. The window was far too small for me to squeeze through, and the iron bars looked sturdy and strong. But there was no glass, and a faint breeze wafted through, smelling of the sea.

I grinned.

I'd never been more grateful for ventilation.

"Echo," I whispered. "Where are you?"

I waited, breath held and gaze glued to the window. Finally, the tiny bat fluttered into the room, slipping between the bars. He hovered in front of me, little eyes black and bright.

Damn, he was cute.

"Can you bring me a tiny piece of the vine that grows in the garden?"

He gave me a skeptical look.

"It's okay if its tiny," I said. "I know you can't carry much."

He bristled, as if offended. Before I could clarify that it was his tiny stature and not his strength that had prompted me to say such an offensive thing, he'd whirled around and sped out the window.

"Please work," I muttered as I began to pace.

Since I had time, I inspected every inch of the dungeon, searching for anything out of the ordinary. There was no telling how many prisoners Hades had locked up here over the years. Maybe one of them had scratched a message in the wall or left something hidden behind a loose stone.

But by the time Echo reappeared, I'd found nothing. It didn't matter, though, because in his little feet, he clutched a tiny sprig of the succulent from the garden.

I grinned at him and took it. "You are a lifesaver."

He made a tiny squeaking noise, then flew up to sit on the windowsill and watch.

I turned to inspect the door, going to my knees to get a better view of the lock set into the wood. No way I'd let this little thing stop me.

I held the vine up to the lock, my heart pounding. This was going to be a tall order for someone who had practiced her magic so little, but I was motivated. As quickly as I could, I fed my magic into it, feeling the power flow from my soul and into the plant. It stretched longer and thinner, growing toward the hole in the lock. When it slipped inside, I reined in my power, no longer asking it to grow. Instead, I directed the tendril to poke around inside the lock, pressing on various tiny steel mechanisms.

At first, my efforts were clumsy, and the vine flopped uselessly inside the lock. I squeezed my eyes shut and focused on my power, trying to get a sense of what the plant could feel, to become one with it. I needed more finesse, something other than a growth spell.

I recalled the brief lesson I'd had with Hades and used what I'd learned to increase my connection with the plant.

It worked.

Unfortunately, it also awoke the darkness deep inside my soul. That hunger grew, the desire for power that made goosebumps rise on my skin.

Was it because I'd learned my tricks from him?

Or was it because of *me*?

At the thought, a desperate sob rose in my throat, coming out of nowhere as the pressure of all that was happening bore down on me.

I sucked it back, swallowing it like a dead fish, and focused on the vine in my hand.

I can do this.

I had to do this.

My magic was good for more than just beating the hell out of people with vines.

And it was working. Eventually, I could feel the different tiny mechanisms like I was touching them myself. Quickly, I used the vine to poke at them, trying to find the pattern that would undo the lock.

Finally, the lock clicked open.

Yes.

I put the vine, now longer and skinnier, into my pocket and stood.

From the window, Echo made a chattering noise.

I grinned back at him. "Pretty good, huh?"

He nodded his tiny head.

I turned back to the door and slipped out into the hall, my heart pounding. It was as dark and dreary as the dungeon behind me, the massive stones covered in a faint slick of damp.

First things first—I tried to reach into the ether to see if I could get the bag that Eve had made for me.

Nothing happened.

"Damn it," I muttered. All that preparation for nothing. It would have been stupid to walk into the underworld emptyhanded, but I'd have preferred if the spell had worked. Now it was just Echo and me, along with whatever magic I could manage.

I inspected the hall. There was no chance I'd navigate out of here on my first try. Hades had taken so many turns that I couldn't remember the way. I turned back to the dungeon, spotting Echo still sitting on the windowsill. "Will you lead me to the back garden?"

He swooped down off the window and out into the hall. I followed, hurrying along on silent feet as we moved through the austere halls. Gradually, wooden floors and dark silk wallpaper replaced the damp stone, and we finally reached the back door.

I'd been here enough times that it was starting to feel like home. The idea made me shudder.

"Thanks, Echo." I pushed open the door, revealing the transformed garden.

Yeah, *this* did not feel like home.

I stared out at the wild vines that snaked along the edges of the huge walled garden, temporarily stunned that I'd created this place. It looked like some kind of haunted wonderland, with the brilliant emerald vines and the deep crimson flowers. Despite the dark night, they somehow glowed with color. Gorgeous, if I were honest with myself.

No.

There was something dark about them. I could feel it. As if they represented the worst of my magic—power-hungry and greedy, selfish and vain.

I tried to ignore them as I hurried out into the garden, racing across the space. The pomegranate tree was no longer there, thank fates. Even if I *was* Persephone, which I was beginning to possibly accept, that was one plant that I couldn't tolerate.

The sky was dark overhead, casting deep shadows through the garden. I stuck to them, keenly aware that I no longer had free roaming privileges like I had last time. Fortunately, Lucifer was nowhere to be seen. My former shadow was probably off guard-dog duty, since Hades thought I was locked away in the dungeon.

Finally, I reached the apothecary's cottage. Purple smoke drifted from the tall stone chimney, and the windows glowed with welcoming light.

Quickly, I knocked on the door, whispering loudly. "Open up. It's me, Seraphia."

4

SERAPHIA

After a few agonizing seconds, the door opened to reveal the apothecary. Her straight black hair gleamed in the light, and her brilliant blue eyes glinted with skepticism. She frowned. "Hi."

"May I come in?"

Her gaze searched the garden behind me, no doubt looking for Hades or Lucifer. Then she relented. "Fine."

I slipped inside, guilt streaking through me. "I'm sorry if I'm putting you at risk with Hades."

She shook her head. "It's fine. He doesn't know you're here."

And he'd better not learn, was the subtext.

I nodded, grateful. "He'll never know."

"Come in." She turned, walking deeper into the house.

I followed her into the main room, almost comforted to be back. The room was far bigger than it looked from the outside. Though it was of average dimensions, the ceiling soared a hundred feet overhead. Dried herbs had been hung from the rafters, their scent filling the space. Fairy lights floated high in the air, lighting the place with a warm glow. Bookshelves climbed to the ceiling, stuffed full of volumes I'd love to get my hands on.

"I like your place," I said.

"Hmm."

The apothecary was the closest thing I had to a friend in the underworld. That might have been Lucifer once, until I'd hit him with an agonizing potion bomb that had melted his chest. That had probably killed what little camaraderie we'd developed.

"Can I get you a drink?" she asked.

"No," I said automatically.

"Come on, you've already had the pomegranate potion. It'll be fine."

She was right. And I really could use one. "I'd kill for a gallon of wine or a case of beer."

She laughed. "I can do you a glass. You need to keep your wits about you."

"True enough."

She disappeared into a room that had to be the kitchen, and I watched the cat who slept by the fire.

There was a lot more to that cat than met the eye, if the magic sparking around him was anything to go by.

"Here." The apothecary returned with the glasses, and I took one.

"Thanks." I clinked it gently against hers, watching the purple liquid gleam within.

"Underworld wine," she said. "A little different."

I took a sip, enjoying the explosion of tart, sweet flavor that burst over my tongue. "It's good!"

"Just about the only thing that's good in this godforsaken place." She collapsed on the long, low couch. "What can I help you with?"

"What's your name?" I couldn't help but ask. Maybe it was rude—she clearly hadn't wanted to tell me all the other times I'd met her. I raised my glass. "We're drinking together. Surely you can tell me."

She frowned, gaze flickering. "Names have power."

I held up a hand. "You're right. I shouldn't have asked. I'm sorry."

She sighed. "It's Alia."

I grinned at her. "Thanks, Alia."

She nodded. "Now, what can I help you with? Because I'm certain you didn't return to the underworld just to say hi to me."

"I need help breaking the pomegranate potion's curse."

She nodded, sipping the wine. "As I thought. You managed to stay away longer than I expected."

I gestured to the front door. "Long enough for that to go wild."

She gave a wry laugh. "It went crazy. I tried to cut it back, but Hades nearly had my head."

"He what?"

"Wouldn't let me cut down your garden."

"That's...unexpected."

She huffed a laugh. "You're telling me. It's your best defense against him, and he let you keep it."

"He needs me on his side," I said.

"He's not afraid of your strength."

"He wants to use it. He wants my help."

"Will you help him?"

"No." I shook my head. "Not a chance in hell. What he wants to do...well, I need to stop it. At all costs."

Alia nodded. "I understand." She tilted her head. "How long ago did you arrive in the underworld?"

I blew out a breath, calculating. "A couple hours ago, at most."

"Hmm."

"What do you mean, *hmm*?"

"Well, the nature of your garden changed right around then. Turned dark."

"What do you mean?"

"The plants used to be pale green with pink flowers. They smelled of something sweet and fresh—best thing to happen to this place since forever—and were soft to the touch. They still bit occasionally, but they weren't so vicious."

My jaw slackened. "And then they became those scary things?"

She nodded. "Yep. The smell went away, and the colors transformed. They must have been responding to the change in you."

"Damn." I sipped the wine, my mind racing. "I felt the darkness grow inside me when I arrived back here. It's a greedy thing, after power and pleasure."

"Bet it feels great."

I nodded, sick to my stomach. "It does. Like I'm in control. Invincible. Safe."

She shook her head. "Hard to resist something like that."

"I know. Hades doesn't even try."

"There's nothing else for him," Alia said. "He's *made* of the darkness. Literally. Like evil given form. There's nothing for him to resist because he can't possibly be any different than he is. There's no other side of him."

"You're wrong," I blurted.

Her brows shot up. "Really?"

I stepped back. Shit. "I mean...yeah, you're wrong. He's not all darkness."

"That's news to me. It'll be news to everyone."

"I *felt* the goodness in him. It's there, just buried so deep no one's ever seen it. He fights it."

"No surprise. You can't have a king of hell with a soft side."

"I never said it was soft." Even that goodness was hard. A bright, pure light of truth. Not *soft.*

"Well, whatever it is, see what you can do about bringing out more of it."

"I can't do that. I won't be here long enough."

She raised her brows. "Sure."

"That's why I came. I need your help with the pomegranate potion."

"I don't know how to undo that."

"I *need* to get out of here, Alia." I said, desperation in my voice. "I almost killed Lucifer with my magic. The darkness made me go crazy."

Her brows rose. "Really?"

A memory flashed—there was something between the two of them. I wanted to prod, but now wasn't the time. Not when so much was at stake.

"Really," I said. "It took me over. And it will keep doing that. I'm not the person to save Hades or bring him to the light. He's just as likely to bring me to the dark."

"Two halves of a whole," she said.

I didn't like the sound of that. It was so...fated. So final. "No. Just two different people who should have nothing to do with each other."

"Well, to me, it sounds like you have two problems: the pomegranate potion and your magic. You need to get control of it. That will keep you from going under his spell."

She was right. I did need control. "Does my lack of control have anything to do with the person who bound my magic?"

On one of my previous visits, she'd told me that my power had been bound, but she hadn't mentioned much more.

"No, I don't think so."

"You really don't know who bound it? I'm *really* Persephone?"

"Of course you are. Denying it now"—she gestured to the garden, as if to illustrate her point—"is just you being obtuse."

"Fine. I am a goddess." The words sounded insane. I didn't even believe them. "But without a goddess's power."

"Oh, you have it, just buried deep inside. Bound by someone or something that I don't know."

"So I have to unlock it."

"One day, yeah. For now, you need to get control of what you have. If you managed to unlock the rest of your power before you gain control, it would be like hooking up a fire hydrant to a garden hose. It would blow you apart."

I grimaced. "Blow me apart?"

She shrugged. "Yeah. Not the most eloquent descrip-tion, but...yeah." She pointed to the garden. "Not to mention, your lack of control is why that happened. And it will keep happening, only worse."

"How do I get control of my magic, then?"

"Hades."

"Nope."

She nodded. "Only a god can teach another god to control their magic. So you need his help."

I slumped back on the couch and stared up at the ceiling. Damn it. "What about the pomegranate potion? Anything you can do there?"

"No way. Even if I could, it's too risky for me."

I nodded, understanding. Hades would kill her if he knew she'd helped me escape. I'd hoped she'd know a way I could fix it, but if not, I'd just have to accept it. Pushing it would be a real jerk move.

"But..." Her voice was soft.

My head swiveled to look at her. "What?"

"If you can give one of the pomegranates from the tree that poisoned you to a potion master on the outside, maybe they'd have a chance."

Eve.

She hadn't been able to do anything before, but she hadn't had a pomegranate from the tree that had poisoned me.

Too bad I'd torn it out of the ground.

That doesn't mean it's gone.

I sat upright. "I need to go."

She nodded. "The tree is in the far corner of the

garden. There's some pieces that haven't been pulverized."

I swallowed hard, remembering the rage that had overtaken me. I definitely had to get that under control.

I gulped the last of my wine—it wasn't a lot, and a girl needed all the courage she could get—and stood. "Thank you, Alia. I really appreciate it."

She nodded. "Anytime. And be safe out there."

"Sure." There was nothing safe about what was happening in the underworld, but there was nothing else I could say.

I left Alia's place and stepped back out into my garden. It was terrible and beautiful all at once. Even though the plants were meant to be the embodiment of darkness, they were still gorgeous.

As I walked through the garden, headed toward the back where the fallen pomegranate was supposed to be, the vines seemed to sway toward me. I tried to ignore them, but it was impossible. They were part of me, and just being near them lit up something inside my soul. I'd been hiding from my magic for so long that it was all trying to rush to the surface.

"Get it together," I muttered, shoving aside the thought.

Echo swooped in front of my face, no doubt drawn by my voice. I looked up at him. "Didn't realize you were following."

He made a soft chattering noise.

"You've got a good view from up there. Can you lead me to the pomegranate tree that I destroyed?"

He chattered, then swooped away. I followed, hurrying through the garden, wanting to get the pomegranate seed before Hades saw me.

A few moments later, Echo flew low over the ground. I found him sitting on a broken branch. Pulverized wood chips were scattered around, and tiny black lizards were feasting on the remains of the smashed pomegranates.

Crap! I waved at them. "Shoo! Go away!"

Echo gave a delighted little screech and swooped after them, driving them away.

"Thanks, buddy." I stood amongst the wreckage I had created and felt a streak of guilt.

I'd done this.

I'd been pissed, but that was no reason to destroy a beautiful tree like this.

I knelt and ran a hand over the bark. "I'm sorry."

Nothing happened, of course.

I shook my head and searched for an intact pomegranate. They'd all been crushed, but I did find a handful of the seeds. These were messy from the juicy red flesh, but beggars couldn't be choosers.

Quickly, I drew a little knife from my pocket and flipped it open. Before I'd met Hades, I hadn't carried a weapon, and I wasn't the sort to carry a big one. But I'd started carrying this one around as soon as I'd returned to Guild City.

I lifted up my sweater and cut off a small square of fabric from my undershirt, then tucked the seeds inside it and folded the fabric closed.

"Echo?" I looked around for him, then spotted him swooping down toward me. I held the seeds up. "Can you hide these for me? I'll need them when I'm able to leave here."

He took the tiny pouch from my hands and gripped it in his feet. I didn't know when I'd have a chance to get to Eve, but I'd make sure it was soon. In the meantime, I didn't want anyone finding me with pomegranate seeds on my person.

Finished, I stood and wiped my juice-stained hands on my jeans. It made me shudder just to have the stuff on my skin, but I hadn't ingested it, so no harm done.

Mind buzzing, I walked back through the garden. The scents and sounds lulled me into a near trance. The pleasure of being in my creation was intense. I brushed my fingertips across the plants, feeling the magic flow into me. Power followed, bringing strength and confidence and dark joy.

Yes.

It felt so good.

At the back of my mind, I dimly knew that this was a dangerous path. This magic wasn't pure and bright, but rather shadowed and dark. Not necessarily evil—I'd have to actually *do* evil with it for it to be evil—but it was still steeped in power and greed and strength.

And I *had* done evil with it. I'd nearly killed Lucifer.

As if he'd heard me thinking about him, his voice drifted over me. "Well, well. If it isn't my new nemesis."

I turned, spotting the beautiful fallen angel striding toward me. His golden hair gleamed, despite the dark night, and his eyes glinted with something I couldn't identify.

"Lucifer." My heart raced with the slightest tinge of fear.

A shark's smile tugged up at the corner of his lips. "You're afraid."

"Am not." I swallowed hard.

He stopped in front of me, all lean strength and broad shoulders. His eyes drifted to Alia's cottage, then back to me.

"Are you mad at me?" I asked. "I almost killed you."

"That's all right. I liked it." His smile was smooth.

"You liked almost dying?"

"Don't knock it 'til you've tried it." The strangest thing was, he sounded genuine. What was his life like, if he thought that? "Now, tell me what you're doing out of your cell."

"I'm looking for Hades." As much as I didn't want to, it was my only choice.

"Well, isn't that convenient? I'm off to see him as well. Shall we walk together?"

5

*H*ADES

As usual of late, the library provided no refuge.

I stared at the books in front of me, unseeing. The leather spines and gold text of the titles blurred together. I'd come to one of the many small libraries in the castle, choosing one dedicated to war strategy. It was generally a favorite, and I'd committed most of the volumes to memory. Still, I'd thought to find inspiration for how to approach Seraphia. I needed her help, as much as I hated to admit it. Her *willing* help. This was not something I could force her to do. Therefore, ours was a battle of wits and will.

Normally, this library would be the perfect starting

point for such an endeavor. And yet, every volume looked as dull as dust.

You don't read fiction?

Seraphia's words echoed in my mind. It'd been weeks since she'd spoken them, yet I could still hear her voice exactly as it had sounded. That voice haunted me, along with her scent. Her taste.

I'd never had any interest in stories that were not true, yet she seemed to enjoy them.

Why the hell did I care?

Fortunately, I heard footsteps in the hall outside.

A distraction. Just what I needed.

I turned toward the door, sensing her magic before I saw her. That fresh scent of flowers, accompanied by the feel of a gentle breeze. My heart sped, pounding against my ribs. I felt my fists clench, an unconscious reaction.

There were so many unconscious reactions around her.

The door swung open, and Lucifer enter, followed by Seraphia. The devil grinned cockily. "Look what I found wandering the premises."

I looked at her, hating that I was the slightest bit impressed. "You escaped."

"You underestimated me. Again."

I had, and the knowledge shamed me. The hot burn of it was uncomfortable. Certainly unfamiliar. I wasn't sure that I'd ever felt such a thing before. The mere idea of feeling anything at all was enough to turn my stomach. Yet actually *doing* it, and feeling an emotion as stupid as shame?

It was unforgivable.

"I won't make that mistake a second time." I strode toward her. "In fact, you're not going to leave my sight."

She quirked a brow. "Ever?"

"Ever."

"Not even when you sleep?"

"I'll chain you to me." The idea made my heart race and my blood heat, two horribly human symptoms that I needed to eradicate at once.

"That's my cue." Lucifer backed out of the room, closing the door behind him.

Suddenly, I was alone with Seraphia. Some of my initial rage had faded, leaving room for a clearer head. My mind immediately went to memories of her. Memories of touching her. Tasting her.

She backed up, gaze wary. "Don't look at me like that."

The heat that I felt had to be reflected on my face. I clenched my jaw and schooled my features. "Better?"

"I prefer you as a block of ice, so yes." She crossed her arms. "Your chaining plan is not going to work."

"I'm sure I can find a way."

"I'm going to assume you are joking." Irritation flashed on her face, and her will of steel glinted in her eyes. "I'm not your pawn, Hades. I've proved that once, and you're not going to enjoy it if I need to prove it again."

Her strength blazed, and I *liked* it.

Heat flared within me.

As the god of this realm, every single being within it bowed before me.

She didn't.

And fates help me, I liked it.

The pleasure of it streaked across my nerve endings, hot and wild. I turned and strode toward the window, desperate for the fresh air.

How did she control my body like this, without so much as a touch? For millennia, I had been in control. Then she arrived...

The large window was open, providing a view of the restless midnight sea. Waves crashed far below, and the wind carried the scent of the ocean. Still, it couldn't drive the smell of her from my memory. It had imprinted on me, permanently becoming part of my soul.

I rested my hand on the window and leaned out. For the briefest moment, the sight of the sea calmed my mind. Then the memory of a similar scene flashed in my mind. I'd kissed her on a windowsill just like this. The things we'd done...

Fates.

Heart thundering, I spun around to face her. There

was no place safe from her, so I might as well look at her. "Why are you here?"

"I'm willing to learn my magic."

Understanding dawned. "You need a teacher."

"Yes, like before."

This was perfect. More than I could have hoped for. Yes, it was dangerous to train her to learn a magic that could defy even mine. But she *had* to learn that magic to help me with my goals.

And I was going to turn her to my side, anyway. I needed a queen.

I felt the corners of my lips tug upward. It was an almost entirely unfamiliar sensation. "I want something in exchange."

"You were willing to help me before."

"I was. But you didn't want my help before. Now you do. So I want something in exchange."

"Bastard."

"I never had a mother. Can't possibly be a bastard."

"I didn't mean literally."

Again, the corners of my lips tugged up. I frowned. Fates, it was strange to smile. I forced the thought away. "I need you to help me find something."

"What?"

"Don't worry about that."

"Of course I'm going to worry about that." She crossed her arms. "And how do I even know you'll live up to your end of the bargain? Will you take more of the potion that compels you to keep your word?"

"No. I'll train you first. Then you'll help me."

She scowled. "How do you know I'll keep *my* word?"

"I'll make you."

She hissed.

I shrugged. "I'm already taking a risk. I know you're trying to learn your magic so that you can lean closer into the light and avoid the dark. So that you can escape."

"Of course."

"I'm confident I can win you to my side."

"You can't."

A low laugh rumbled from my throat, and I strolled toward her. My skin lit with anticipation as I neared, stopping right in front of her. I didn't dare touch—if I did, there was no telling where I'd stop—but the tension that tightened between us felt like a caress. "You've felt the lure. The pleasure of the dark."

Her jaw tightened, but the knowledge glinted in her eyes. I'd seen it in her when she'd been strangling Lucifer with her vines. She was fighting it even now.

"I've no idea what you're talking about."

I leaned close, my lips nearly touching her neck as I breathed deeply of her scent. Desire shot through me, and I knew I was playing with fire.

"You will," I whispered at her ear.

She shuddered so hard, I could see it run over her. I

stepped back, needing to escape her scent if I was going to keep my wits about me.

"Fine," she said. "I'll help you with your mystery search. *If* you also allow my friends to visit. And if you won't try to stop me from visiting them in Guild City."

I blinked at her.

She was serious.

Seraphia

I stared up at Hades, my mind racing.

"You're looking at me like I've asked you to build a roller coaster through hell," I said.

"Friends? Here?" His brows rose.

"Yes, friends. Are you familiar with the concept?" Even as I said the words, I knew he wasn't. Lucifer had said as much last time I'd been here. He'd called Hades his friend but admitted that Hades considered no one a friend.

He's not human.

This was a good reminder. He was literally not human, so why would he have a thing like friends?

His jaw worked for a moment as he decided how he would answer me.

"Give in," I said.

I needed him to agree to at least one of my demands so that I could give the pomegranate seeds to Eve. But more than that, I wanted to see my friends. It wasn't like I was going to invite them over for girls' nights, but having Eve visit as a raven wouldn't be so bad.

Worry hit me. I held up a hand. "*And* if they come, you can't poison them with your darkness the way you did Mac."

"I have no idea why you want this."

"You wouldn't understand." Something flickered on his face, an expression I couldn't quite identify, but I pressed onward. "Remember, I *can* leave."

"It tears you apart."

"I *know*." That familiar anger surged, and I stepped back.

He shook his head. "You're my prisoner, so no, this is not happening."

I laughed. "Prisoner? Hardly. We're equals now, Hades, whether you like it or not."

"Not quite."

He was right. We *weren't* equals. He was a damned god, for fates' sake.

So are you, the little voice whispered inside me. I was supposed to be Persephone, but I didn't feel like it.

"You need my help," I said. "And you saw the vision of your end goal. We walk side by side toward that, and I go willingly." I never would, but the words were enough to make interest gleam in his eyes.

"Fine." He nodded sharply, clearly reluctant. "You may have what you ask for because I know you'll be required to return. But while you're here, you'll be watched by me or by Lucifer."

"Sure, sure." Now that I had his acquiescence, I wanted to move on. "What next?"

"We'll leave at dawn for your first training session."

"Where are we going?"

"A forest. The only forest of decent size."

A forest. Excitement thrummed within me. "All right. See you in the morning."

I turned to go, heading toward the door.

"And where do you think you're going?" his voice rumbled from behind me.

I turned back and scowled. "To my chamber."

"No, you're not. You're coming to mine."

"No."

"You're coming, or I'll carry you."

"You cannot be serious."

"I'm not going to underestimate you anymore. So unless you want me to actually chain you to me, you'll sleep in my quarters."

I glared at him, debating. He really would carry me there. He'd already carried me to the dungeon. I gestured to him. "Lead on, then."

He nodded and strode from the library, leading me through the castle and to his quarters. When we arrived, he gestured to the couch in front of the bookshelves in the main room. It looked pristine and new, as if he'd never so much as sat on it.

I was fairly sure he hadn't.

At least it was better than his bed. "This will do."

He nodded. "Make yourself comfortable. Dinner will be delivered soon."

Food.

My stomach grumbled at the thought. I could technically eat food from the underworld, now that I'd had the pomegranate potion. It wouldn't force me to stay here any more than the potion had.

Hades turned on his heel and disappeared into his sleeping chambers. His presence felt like a weight disappearing from the room, and I couldn't help but rub my arms.

Unfortunately, it was an oddly lonely feeling. He had me on edge any time he was near, but it was a *good* edge, almost. Like I enjoyed the excitement of being near him, no matter how dangerous he was.

And no matter what, it was impossible to forget what we'd had together when I'd been here last. Just a few stolen moments while my mind was fogged, but they'd been amazing.

I slumped on the couch, staring at the ceiling. Now what?

Echo fluttered inside to land on my shoulder, his weight so faint that I could barely feel him. His presence was a comfort, though. He no longer had the little pouch of pomegranate seeds, so I assumed he'd stashed them somewhere as I'd asked.

"How are you, buddy?"

He didn't answer, but he settled down to sleep on my shoulder. My mind raced with everything I'd learned since I'd come here, and everything that I was going to have to do.

Find a way to leave permanently.

Master my magic so I didn't lose my mind.

Save Hades.

I jerked.

Where had that last thought come from? He couldn't *be* saved. Why the hell would I even try?

Because I wanted to. Fates, how I wanted to. I'd seen the conflict in him. The faint flashes of goodness—very faint, but there.

A knock sounded on the door.

Thank fates, a distraction. "Food!" I sat upright.

Echo rustled on my shoulder and made an annoyed chattering noise.

"Oh, don't complain," I said. "I'm sure there's something tasty there for you."

I could feel his interest like it was my own, and the connection between us was a comforting blanket wrapped around my soul. As long as Echo was here, I wasn't alone.

Quickly, I went to the door and opened it. Kerala, the

maid who'd helped me last time I'd been here, stood with a tray in her hands. Her eyes flared wide. "Seraphia. I knew you were back, but I didn't expect to see you here."

"No?" I took the heavy tray from her.

"Not in his quarters." Surprise flickered in her eyes. "No one is ever in here but him."

Of course they weren't. The mere concept of *friends* confused him. "Well, I won't be here for long."

"Going to try to escape again?"

"You know me too well, Kerala." I nodded to the food piled high on the tray. "Thank you for this."

She nodded, then disappeared. I carried the tray to the table and looked at it, debating. There were steamed, colorful vegetables piled next to grilled meat and crusty bread. Fruits and cakes, wine and water.

I sighed, debating.

Then my stomach grumbled so loudly I should have been embarrassed.

Screw it.

I reached for a piece of bread and held it up. "Is this going to do me in, Echo?"

I tilted my head to look at him out of the corner of my eye, and he shook his little head.

"Good." I took a huge bite and watched Echo while I chewed. He darted toward the fruit basket, grabbed a grape, and flew off.

I kept chewing the bread. It was good, but not great.

Probably because it was from the underworld, where everything kind of sucked by its very nature.

Except Hades.

Ugh.

Stupid thought.

Of course he sucked. It was hard to imagine such a boring, modern word being applied to him.

Where was he, anyway?

I strolled toward the bedroom, curiosity dragging me forward. It was probably stupid to corner the lion in his den, but I was determined not to be afraid.

I was no dummy, though. Of course I was afraid.

Still, I'd try.

Fake it 'til you make it.

Silently, I slipped into the massive space. He wasn't in the huge bed, which was made with military precision. I looked away from it, unwilling to imagine him sleeping, then turned toward another door.

It was open, revealing a large bathroom. In the center, a sunken tub was built right into the stone floor. It was more like a pool, ten feet by ten feet and full of steaming water.

Hades stood in the middle of it, broad shoulders and lean waist rising above the surface. Steam curled around his damp hair and drifted over muscles hewn by war.

My breath caught in my throat at that sight of his smooth skin, beaded with water. I stared at him dumbly for a moment, blinking as I took it all in. I'd seen him without a shirt before, and the sight had been just as stunning then. But I'd never seen his back. Not from this angle.

Beneath his dark tattoos, scars striped across his skin, looking like someone had taken a dull knife to him and then poured salt on the wound.

I bit my lip, clenching my fists to keep from reaching out to him.

It was none of my business.

But I hadn't seen them before, even though I'd kissed his back so briefly. Had he hidden them with magic?

Now they were revealed. He didn't want me to see them.

I stepped backward, desperate to escape. I couldn't take the pounding of the blood through my veins. Didn't want him to turn and find me staring at him.

Silently, I hurried back to the living room and stared at the bookshelf.

What had happened to him?

Torture.

The word echoed in my head, but it was ridiculous. He was one of the top three gods of Greek myth. No one was higher than him. Some of the myths said Zeus was at the top, but I'd seen them fight. They were equals.

It should be impossible to wound a god like that. He should have healed.

Why hadn't he?

I rubbed my arms, my mind racing. There was so much more to him than met the eye. So much more than I knew. It made me want to know him better.

To help him.

No.

I was being a damned ninny.

No matter what had happened to him, he'd proved how dangerous he was. And I'd seen what he was after. It was deadly.

The minutes ticked by, and I felt the bedroom door close more than heard it. I turned to it, confirming my suspicions.

He wasn't coming out for food. It was time to go to sleep. I didn't know what was coming tomorrow, but I'd need my strength for it, I was sure.

Slowly, I turned back to the couch. My gaze snagged on the section of bookshelf that contained *The Oresteia.*

His favorite book.

I'd taken a copy but hadn't had time to read it.

Lie.

I'd had time. Sort of. I just hadn't wanted to. I was already too drawn to the deadly, evil god. The last thing I needed was to get to know him better.

I climbed onto the couch. There was no blanket, of course. Little things like throw blankets and decorative pillows were *not* Hades' style.

Still, it was warm enough as I slowly drifted off to sleep, memories of Hades dancing in my mind.

6

SERAPHIA

The next morning, I woke with a blanket thrown over me.

I frowned.

Hades?

It was too big for Echo to have carried.

But Hades was nowhere to be seen. His quarters were completely empty—I could feel his absence.

I rose, pulling on my boots and vowing to get a bath after this first training session was done. Echo was gone as well, but a tray of breakfast sat on the table. I ate quickly, fueling up for whatever was to come. Again, I tried to reach into the ether to retrieve the bag that Eve had given me.

It didn't work.

Damn.

At least I still had the sprigs of plants in my pocket. They were useful for a lot.

I turned toward the door just as it opened. Hades stood on the other side, dressed in the sturdier dark metal armor that he'd worn last time we'd left his city.

His dark eyes met mine. "Are you ready?"

I nodded. "How far are we going?"

"Not far. An hour on Horse."

"We need to take Horse?" I frowned, not liking the idea of being pressed up against him. It'd been bad enough the first time. and that had been before we'd really kissed. Now that I had that memory in my head, I couldn't handle the idea. "I want my own horse."

"You're joking."

"I'm not."

"Can you ride?"

Not really. "Yes."

"That's a lie."

"Get me my own horse. I'll be fine. I'm a damned goddess, for fates' sake."

"You embrace it now?"

"Admit it, not embrace it. And I want my own horse. I'm not sitting pressed up against you."

Something flickered in his gaze, and he nodded. "All right. Come with me."

I followed him out of the room and down the hall.

Despite his massive size, his footsteps were silent on the stone floor. I tried to match him, not wanting to be the clumsy one of the pair.

"So, you don't want to fly to the forest?" I asked, already knowing the answer but wanting the *why*.

He stiffened slightly, the movement barely perceptible from the corner of my eye.

"Why do you hate your wings so much?"

"I don't hate my wings."

If I'd thought his posture was stiff, his voice put that to shame. "Of course you do. You never use them. On the rare instances you do, you put them right back where they came from as soon as you're done."

"They're not useful."

"That's total bollocks, and you know it. They're *wings*, for fates' sake. You can soar above the clouds."

"I have no interest in the clouds."

"Hmm." There was so much there that he wasn't telling me. But we'd reached the main entry hall of the castle, so there was no time to ask. Not that I thought he'd answer me.

We strode toward the door. Hades stopped in front of one of the guards, telling him to fetch a horse for me.

Together, we walked out into the murky daylight of the underworld. As before, it was gray and dreary, with no sun cutting through the clouds and a faint smell of smoke on the air.

Hades led the way down the stairs, taking them two

at a time, and stopped in front of Horse, who stood patiently at the base.

I joined him, staring up at the big animal. It ignored me, too regal for the likes of me.

A few moments later, a gleaming ebony horse was led toward the stairs from the side of the castle. It was elegant and tall, with a mane shot through with something that flickered like flame.

I swallowed hard, suddenly regretting my decision to request my own horse.

How hard could it be, though?

The servant stopped in front of me, and I eyed the saddle. Just as I was debating how to get onto it, I felt Hades' strong hands grip my waist. They burned in the best way, sending a shiver through me. He lifted me up, and I swung my leg over the saddle. His hands tightened slightly on my waist, as if he didn't want to let go, and then he released me.

"Thanks." I gripped the reins and looked down at him, spotting the heat in his gaze.

Even that little touch lit us both up.

He's never touched anyone else.

I was dead certain of it. So of course it lit him up. It had nothing to do with me and everything to do with the fact that I was the first.

In front of me, Hades mounted Horse smoothly, then gave the animal a slight nudge in the sides with his heels. I mimicked the movement, and my mount picked up the pace.

Horse moved at a swift clip away from the castle. Hades rode like he'd been doing it for thousands of years—which he probably had. He was one with the beast, his form elegant and controlled.

My mount followed. I patted the creature's neck, still having no idea if it was a male or a female, and leaned over. "I'm going to call you Sally, okay?"

The horse whinnied, and I took that as an *okay*.

Sally picked up the pace to join Horse, and the two creatures trotted side by side as we passed the dark stone buildings that lined the street. I couldn't help but wonder if Hades had given me a magical horse that knew exactly what to do, because this was way too easy. It was coming in handy, that was for sure.

As we rode through the city, people came out of their houses to watch. The crown appeared at Hades' head, the symbol that he only wore in front of his people. When their gazes turned toward me, there was something almost like reverence in their eyes.

I twitched. It felt weird to be the recipient of such a stare.

One by one, they bowed. For Hades, of course. But their eyes were also on me. And when I look at Hades, he appeared pleased. It was just the faintest difference to the set of his mouth that gave me the impression, and it could have been total bollocks.

I shivered and focused forward, not liking what it implied if the citizens really were bowing to me. In all of the myths that humans told about Hades, Persephone became his wife.

His wife.

No way. It was crazy to even think it.

I shook away the thought and focused on not falling off of Sally. We passed torture square, and I winced at the sight of the people hanging there. The memory of Kerala telling me about their crimes flashed through me.

They deserved it.

I knew they did, but still...

I hated looking at them.

We neared the turnoff for the city gates, and I looked toward the huge library that connected to Guild City. At the base of the steps, I spotted the night wolves. They lurked in the shadows, their eyes on me.

Instead of feeling fear, I felt a connection. Somehow, with magic I still didn't understand, I'd been able to control them. Just like Hades.

We passed under the massive gate and exited the city, swiftly descending the mountainside. Hades directed Horse toward the cliffs overlooking the sea, and Sally followed. I tried to focus on becoming a better rider, but Sally was in such control that it didn't really matter. I just had to hang on.

We rode along the coast for what felt like hours,

though it was probably shorter. The sea crashed below, the saltwater smell glorious and similar to the beach back on earth. I couldn't imagine what monsters lurked in these depths, however.

In the distance, I spotted the same forest that I'd seen last time we'd left the city in pursuit of the Temple of Shadows.

"Is that where we're going?" I asked.

"Yes."

A few minutes later, we turned away from the sea and cut across the planes. The forest called to me, its song stronger and stronger as we grew nearer. I could feel the life there, vibrant and fresh...but it didn't feel quite right.

As we neared, I saw why.

The forest was struggling. Ancient oaks grew out of the ground, a hundred feet tall if they were an inch. Despite their size, half of them looked dead, and the other half seemed like they were almost there.

"Have they always looked like this?" I asked as Sally and Horse stopped about forty feet away.

"Yes." Hades surveyed them with an impassive gaze. "But it's the strongest, biggest forest we have."

I studied the sturdy trunks and twisted branches, the leaves that decorated only half the trees. Even those were falling at an alarming rate. Some scrubby grasses and a few bushes grew on the forest floor between the trees, but it was relatively barren.

The entire place made me sad.

I shoved away the thought and turned to Hades. "Now what?"

"We go in. We'll practice. You'll feel your power unlock when you've gained control. It will be very distinct. You won't miss it."

I nodded, my gaze on the trees. I could feel animal life as well, now that I focused on it. Like I had a sixth sense for the heartbeats of smaller creatures.

"What else lives in this forest?" I asked.

"Rabbits, wolves, rodents. Not many, but they are there."

"Was the underworld always so miserable and dark?"

He looked at me sharply, but it wasn't offense I saw in his gaze. He wasn't the sort to become offended—he was too confident, and he didn't actually care what anyone else thought, from what I could tell. Instead, he looked curious, as if I'd asked a question whose answer he should know, but realized he didn't.

"I'm not sure," he said, confirming my suspicions. His jaw set, and his gaze closed down. "Come. We'll practice."

He directed Horse toward the middle of the forest, and I followed, Sally picking her way between the trees. We reached a clearing, and Hades dismounted gracefully.

I tried to mimic his movements, but my foot got tangled up in the stirrup. My stomach pitched, and I was about to lose my grip when his strong hands gripped my waist.

Embarrassment burned through me as he helped me down. I vowed to learn to do this better.

After he set me on the ground, I turned. "Thanks."

He nodded. "Are you ready?"

"Yeah. But I don't know what for."

"Come." He gestured for me to follow him deeper into the forest. After a moment's walk, he stopped in the middle of a circular clearing surrounded by huge oaks. They soared overhead, their twisted breaches reaching toward the sky, forming a cage around us.

I stopped in front of him and looked up, trying not to be caught in his gaze. There was something about looking right at him that made my mind go a bit fuzzy. But I couldn't afford to lose my focus, especially if he was going to touch me.

Hades

Seraphia looked up at me, her gaze set and determined. She was tiny but fierce. I'd known it ever since I'd first started watching her.

But she'd grown even stronger in her time away from me. Even more determined.

I liked it. I liked when she showed her spine of steel and refused to back down.

It was odd to admit to *liking* anything. As with emotion, *liking* things or finding pleasure in them was entirely strange.

And she seemed to ignite the most emotion of all. Even my people had been able to see what she was. They'd been bowing to her as much as to me, and the sight had filled me with a strong sense of satisfaction.

"So?" she asked. "How are you supposed to teach me my magic?"

"It's not dissimilar to what we did before. But I'm not teaching so much as I'm helping you access it."

"What do you mean, exactly?"

"I become a conduit for you to access your power. By touching another god, it helps you more effectively find and use your own power."

She nodded. "All right. That's kind of what it felt like before. You'll touch my shoulder?"

"Yes, but you're trying to control more than a small plant this time. You're trying to control the forest." I reached for her shoulder, moving slowly so that she'd see me coming.

She stiffened, watching warily, and I gently gripped her left shoulder. Her body burned under my gloved palm, sending a shiver up my arm. I swallowed hard as I turned her around to face away from me. I rested my hands on each shoulder, standing so close to her that it made my entire body vibrate.

"See what you can do," I said.

She nodded, staring out at the trees. Her hair gleamed in the low light, twisted into a braid that fell down her back. The smell of it seeped into me, making my breath catch as it filled me with warmth. I wanted to lean down and press my face against her neck as I had earlier, drawing deeply of her scent.

No.

That wasn't the purpose of this.

And things like that were enough to steal my focus and turn my mind. Not only did that kind of pleasure make me feel dreadfully human, it turned me away from the dark. The light beckoned when I was with her like that, and this was unacceptable.

"Here goes nothing," she murmured.

Her magic sparked through her, prickling against my palms. I could feel it as she reached deep, trying to wrest it up from within her soul.

I drew in a steady breath and released my own power, feeding it into her, envisioning it traveling down my arms and into her shoulders.

She gasped and swayed, and her magic burned brighter.

In front of us, one of the trees began to move, its

limbs reaching toward the sky. Tiny appeared on the branches, and awe filled me.

She was life.

The opposite of me. I shouldn't be so impressed. But death had been my world for so long that seeing something like this was incredible.

Wonder filled me as I watched the buds appear. Then they stopped, almost forming leaves but not quite.

I could feel her frustration in the tension of her shoulders, in the way her magic flared.

"It's stopped," she said.

"Here." I pulled her toward me, pressing her back fully against my front and wrapping an arm around her waist.

She gasped, the sound sending a fierce spike of pleasure through me. It was nothing compared to the feeling of having her in my arms, however. She was so much smaller than me, yet the memory of her ferocity streaked through me.

"Is this necessary?" she squeaked.

"Yes. If you want to keep that tree growing." And it truly was. Though it felt so good that I might have lied about it just to have more of her.

"Fine."

The closer touch allowed me to funnel more of my magic into her, and she responded in kind, reaching for more of her own. It surged to life within her, vibrant and true.

The fact that I could feel it was astonishing. I knew the theory of this kind of thing—I had read about it in preparation for finding her—but I'd never done it before. Never joined my magic with another's in this way. It was strangely intimate, making me feel like my skin was too raw, but I craved more of it. Craved more of her.

As her magic began to grow within her, the trees responded. Buds appeared on every branch, and the sight of it made me wonder for the first time whether the underworld truly had to look the way it did.

7

Seraphia

Magic flowed through my veins like a drug, the power making me feel like I was flying. Hades' touch burned across every inch of my skin. Desire followed, but I drew in a ragged breath, trying to ignore it as I focused on the trees.

He'd been right. His touch somehow made it easier to access the magic that resided deep in my soul. There was so much more of it than I'd ever realized. So much more of it that I couldn't access, even with his help.

I could feel it, deep inside me. Locked away. *Bound.*

Amala's word echoed in my ears. Someone had bound my magic.

But I couldn't worry about that now. I needed to

worry about these trees. I needed to bring them back to life. They called to me so strongly that I couldn't resist.

I dug deeper, trying to find as much power as I could, and gave it to the trees. Heady delight filled me as I watched them heal. I leaned into it, letting the magic sweep me up. So much power surged through me that my head began to swim. My vision blurred, and my skin tingled as the forest rotated around us. Breathing became difficult, then seemed to stop entirely.

For the briefest second, my vision went dark.

Gasping, I blinked.

My eyes flashed open, but everything looked different.

The trees were the same, but I was standing in another part of the forest. I could no longer feel my body, in fact. All I could feel was the power—pure, heady, dark. It filled me with the most glorious strength and confidence, health and vitality.

I'd never felt so amazing in all my life. I could accomplish *anything.*

I spun around, catching sight of two figures.

Hades and myself.

The sight nearly made me lightheaded.

We just...*fit.*

He stood behind me, tall and broad, with one strong arm wrapped around my waist. I was far shorter than he was, and the way he curved protectively over me made something pulse inside me. It was the only physical sensation I had.

Was this an out-of-body experience?

It had to be.

I'd become one with the magic of the forest. The earthy scent was stronger, the feel of the breeze stronger. I was connected with it in a way I never had been before.

I watched as we stood in the middle of the clearing, seemingly frozen. Magic sparked around us, swirling in glittering bursts of gold and black. The tattoo on my arm glowed as I used my power. Hades was so deadly, so evil, yet the way he held me...

I wanted to watch forever, but the forest called to me. *Needing* me.

I could feel its hunger, its desperation for life. It'd been suffering here for an untold amount of time, but I could fix it. I just needed to give the dying trees the life they so desperately required. And I could feel it in the forest, low against the ground. In the air.

Take.

I commanded the trees with my power, feeling the connection between them and the earth. I commanded their branches and roots to reach out and take the life that they so desperately required. Somehow, it felt dark.

Bad.

But they needed it. And the power felt so good.

I kept going.

When I spotted one of the branches strangling a

silver bird, I gasped. Then I caught sight of a root with a rabbit in its grip.

This was where the trees were getting their life? I'd commanded them to take it from the forest creatures?

Yes.

The darkness seemed to swell inside me, pleased that I was finally making the connection. Despite the fact that the idea made me ill, I *liked* the sensation. I felt invincible, and the trees were as well.

And yet, my soul screamed within me. What I was doing was *terrible*. I'd never do something like this normally, and yet the darkness had control of me. It strangled my normal self, urging me on, filling me with such certainty that I ignored the horror around me and kept going. Kept saving the forest at expense of the animals.

Seraphia!

The shriek sounded inside my head, and I looked up to see Echo in the grip of a branch.

Horror opened a chasm inside my soul, and desperation followed.

The sight of it shocked me into action, dredging up the last vestiges of my soul that fought to embrace the light.

"Stop!" I tried to scream.

But I had no body. I was still an incorporeal mass, watching the trees strangle the life from all the helpless creatures of the forest.

I had to fix this. Had to save them.

They needed life. *All* of them needed life now. The forest animals that were dying and the trees that were just trying to survive. My first attempt at using magic was causing unmitigated chaos, and only I could stop it.

But how?

Where was I going to get that kind of living energy from?

For a long, horrible moment, my mind was entirely blank...and then it came to me.

Myself.

The thought blazed with such certainty that it had to be true.

Head ringing with panic, I tried force my magic into the trees. Into the animals.

At first, it didn't work. The darkness didn't want to let it work. Hades, this place, had twisted me. It'd polluted my soul, and now I had to find the real me again.

"Echo!" The word was soundless, but the bat seemed to understand.

He thrashed more fiercely against the branch, finally breaking free. Frantic, he flew toward me. Toward the shadow that I'd become.

When his little form shot through my chest, I felt a burst of strength. Of focus. He flew back and hovered near my shoulder, his presence strengthening me.

I had no idea how to use my magic like this—I was

certain this wasn't what Hades was training me to do—but I had to try. Desperate, I focused on the forest around me, imagining giving my life force to the trees and animals, envisioning it as a white mist that flowed into them with strength and healing.

Come on.

It had to work. If it didn't, I'd lose myself to the dark. I could feel it even now, pulling on me. It sang to me, a siren song of strength and power. The worst part was that it was nearly impossible to resist.

But I did—barely. I focused on Echo, taking strength from my familiar, and fed my magic into the trees. I imagined it flowing into them as a glowing light of life. Eventually, they released the animals. I felt it more than saw it, but I knew they were fine. Shaken, but alive.

My strength waned as the trees turned greener. The buds unfurled into flowers, and leaves appeared. My vision went blurry, and my thoughts turned slow.

One second, I was standing away from my physical body, and the next, I was inside it. For the briefest moment, I felt Hades' arms around me. I should hate it, knowing the way he'd pushed my magic.

I didn't. Couldn't.

Before I could fully process the thought, unconsciousness reached up to take me. I collapsed, my knees going weak. The last thing I felt before passing out was Hades sweeping me off my feet.

Hades

In my arms, Seraphia collapsed.

"Seraphia!" The fear in my voice would have shocked me if I'd had time to think about it.

Her form had gone completely still, and fear was an icicle through my heart. I swept her up, then went to my knees, cradling her against me. Her face was pale, her cheeks almost hollow.

"Seraphia." I shook her gently, cradling her back with one arm while I brushed the hair off her face with my other hand, wishing I wasn't wearing the glove. "Wake up, Seraphia."

Her breathing was shallow. Too shallow.

I pressed my hand to the middle of her chest, about to heal her.

She gasped, jerking, and her eyes opened. The emerald depths were slightly cloudy with exhaustion and confusion.

"Don't," she croaked.

"Don't heal you?"

"Don't want anything from you."

Pain pierced me, a thin blade of steel through the heart. I blinked at her, surprised by the feeling. She hated me that much.

Of course she did.

"Are the animals all right?" she whispered, trying to sit up. She was too weak, and the movements were barely a twitch.

"They're fine."

"You almost made me kill them." Accusation echoed in her voice.

"I didn't. That was you."

Shadows flashed in her eyes—anger and confusion. Regret. She had to know it was true. I hadn't commanded that. I'd had no idea how she would use her magic, just that I was meant to help her embrace it. She was in control of how she used it.

"This place..." Her words were weak, but she seemed determined to get them out. "The darkness."

"What of it?" My tone was sharp. "The darkness *is* this place. It's the underworld. It's not meant to be anything other than what it is."

Frustration bubbled up within me, worthless, pointless frustration. I was a creature of the underworld, created from death and darkness itself to lead. And yet, she expected the underworld to be different. Expected *me* to be different.

"Don't you see that's impossible?" I asked. "Asking me or the underworld to be anything other than what we are is like asking the earth not to circle the sun."

"Physics again?"

"Fate."

Her lips tightened, and she looked like she wanted to say something. But her eyes fluttered closed, exhaustion seeming to suck her down.

I swallowed hard, staring at her. My chest was a riot of emotion, conflicting feelings battering against each other. It made my head spin. Made me want to rise up and fight something, *anything*, to get this energy out.

But I couldn't. She needed me.

I swallowed the feeling down and rose, trying not to jostle Seraphia. She needed to rest. I carried her to Horse, mounting as smoothly as I could, then nudged him in the sides.

He took off at a smooth walk, and Seraphia's mount followed. Though the walk was slower than my usual preference, it was better for Seraphia.

I held her close, trying not to be swayed by the warmth of her in my arms. It burned, as usual. But I loved it. Far too much.

I could die like this. Happily.

Fates.

These thoughts were insane. She was diverting me from my path, stirring up things that should never happen.

I looked down at her, trying to see her as what she really was—my opponent.

A worthy opponent. Not a pawn.

I wouldn't make that mistake again.

And she'd proved her strength here today. She'd been magnificent.

Unable to help myself, I looked back at the forest.

The enormous trees grew tall and strong, green leaves tipping each branch. It didn't look bright and cheerful, but it was a gem of life in the middle of a sea of death. I'd never seen it like this—not in all my time in the underworld.

And yet, Seraphia had changed it on her first try.

I frowned.

What did this mean for the future? How would she change this place?

How would she change me?

I shook away the thought. She wouldn't change me. *I* would change *her*. She had it in her, the darkness that wanted to rise. She'd been magnificent in the forest. All I had to do was encourage that. Stoke it.

Soon, she'd be willing to help me with anything. We'd walk across the earth together, spreading the dominion of the underworld, as I'd been created to do.

We reached the city gates as the sun was beginning to set. Horse walked sedately through the gates, heading toward the castle. As we made our way down the city streets, people came out of their houses, watching Seraphia and me.

Unable to help myself, I pulled her closer, wanting to put myself between her and their curious gazes. To be helpless in front of your people was a deadly mistake as a ruler, and with every second that passed, I accepted more and more that I wanted her to rule at my side.

Someone as magnificent as Seraphia deserved to be the queen of hell. And if that was my end goal, I didn't want my citizens looking at her in this state.

I glared at them all, leveling a stare that would freeze fire. They scurried back into their houses, and Horse continued on. We reached the castle a few minutes later, and I smoothly took the stairs two at a time, striding past the guards and into my chambers.

In the main room, I stopped, eying the couch. I could put here there. That's where she'd slept last night.

But the bed called to me. She should be there.

I swallowed hard at the mere idea.

I wanted her. Of course I did. Though I'd never wanted another in all my days, I wanted her. She burned me like fire, and I wanted to become one with the blaze. It was dangerous. I knew it.

I didn't care.

Decided, I strode toward the bedroom. The massive bed awaited, empty as ever. It had never bothered me before. Never so much as registered in my mind that it shouldn't be that way.

Now, it did.

I laid her on the bed and removed her shoes, then pulled the covers up over her.

The sight of her in my bed, pale and beautiful, made

a fist clench at my heart. I stepped back, nearly tripping over my feet.

Too much.

This was too much.

I whirled around and stalked from the room, seeking the darkness at the base of my castle. The abyss called to me, offering sweet oblivion.

I would take it.

Now, more than ever, I needed to recommit myself to my cause. There was no other option. I'd been born for this. It didn't matter what Seraphia inspired within me. My goal was all that mattered. All that *could* matter.

8

Seraphia

I woke in a massive bed, alone. A blanket was pulled up over me, and a pillow rested under my cheek.

Groggy, I blinked and sat up. What had happened? I didn't actually remember getting into bed. And whose bed was this?

Confused, I looked around—and it came to me.

Hades.

This was his sleeping chamber. My heart thundered as I turned toward his side of the bed. I'd felt alone when I'd woken, but what if I wasn't?

What if I hadn't been?

Could I have really slept next to Hades and not known it?

But the bed was empty, the covers undisturbed.

He hadn't been here. Somehow, I knew it. I would have woken in the night if he'd climbed in bed with me. No matter how ill or unconscious, I wouldn't have been able to ignore something like that.

So where was he? And what time was it?

I looked toward the window and spotted the pale gray light of daytime. Or at least, I thought it was daytime. It was so hard to tell in the underworld, where it was just different shades of misery.

Still tired, I climbed from the bed. "Hades?" I called, even though I could feel he wasn't in his quarters.

There was no answer, of course.

The waistband of my jeans dug into my hip, and I realized I'd gone to bed fully dressed. Hades must have done that.

I couldn't help but appreciate the courtesy of it. Fates knew I would have freaked the hell out if he'd undressed me. My shoes sat near the end of the bed, but I really didn't want to put them on. Not until I'd had a bath.

I needed fresh clothes, too.

As if answering my call, there was a knock on the door. I strode to it and opened it, finding Kerala on the other side. Hades must have sent her. The pretty maid smiled and held out a change of clothes. All black, as usual for this dreary place.

"Thank you, Kerala." I took them. "Do you know where Hades is?"

"Couldn't say, no."

"Thanks."

She curtsied and left. I turned back to the room and spotted breakfast on the table. I set the clothes down on a chair and picked up a pastry. As I bit in, I couldn't help the anxiety that streaked through me. Though I knew rationally that eating shouldn't make any difference since I'd already had the pomegranate potion, I'd spent so long being afraid of it.

Tasted good, though. Not phenomenal, but I doubted anything tasted phenomenal here.

Except Hades.

The traitorous thought made me want to hiss.

Instead, I went to the bathroom, desperately wanting a bath. The chamber was large, and the bathing pool drew my eye. It was set directly into the dark stone ground, massive and full of steaming water. A huge window overlooked the sea, but I had eyes only for the swimming pool–sized tub.

Quickly, I shoved the rest of the pastry into my mouth, then shucked my clothes and climbed into the water. It closed around me, warm and lovely, and I sighed. Besides the apothecary's cottage, it was the only nice place I'd been in all of this miserable underworld. Except the forest. That had been all right once I'd fixed it.

I didn't have time to linger, but I wanted to.

I'll come back.

There. That was a compromise.

I forced myself to bathe efficiently, limiting myself to only two laps of the gorgeous pool.

Clean, I rose up, shivering as the chill air replaced the warmth. As quickly as I could, I dried myself off and changed into clean clothes. The room echoed hollowly as I moved, feeling distinctly empty without Hades' commanding presence.

Echo fluttered through the window and sat on top of the fruit basket, watching me with keen eyes. Though the room didn't feel quite as empty now, he was no substitute for Hades.

Fully dressed, I looked at Echo, my mind spinning. "Well, what now?"

He said nothing. In the forest, I thought he'd called my name. Maybe he didn't talk.

That didn't mean I couldn't talk to him.

"Hades has gone somewhere unknown," I said. "So I think this is my best shot at getting a pomegranate to Eve in Guild City."

Echo nodded, but skepticism glinted in his eyes.

"You're worried about Hades going back on the bargain, aren't you?" He'd said I could go back, but... "I agree. He's not trustworthy. Can you get me the pomegranate seeds I gave you, then sneak me through the city? Take the back roads to the library?"

Echo nodded, then launched himself off the fruit bowl and swooped out of the room. As I waited for him to return with the seeds, I paced Hades' room, inspecting the bookshelves. The topics ranged from strategy to war to history. Not a single novel in sight.

He didn't enjoy anything, did he?

Didn't know how.

I shook the thought away. I shouldn't care.

Echo returned and dropped the small pouch in my hand. I closed my fist around the juice-stained fabric. "Thanks."

He fluttered around and left the room, squeaking to call me along.

I followed him through the castle, careful to stick to the shadows. I wasn't going to let anyone stop me, but I'd rather not deal with the confrontation.

We were lucky. Or maybe it was Echo. I got the impression he had a second sense for avoiding people, and we made it into the back garden without incident.

The sight of the place shocked me anew, the vines growing wild and free. And dark. The magic that radiated from them was distinctly evil.

And they're part of me.

The horror of it made me want to vomit.

Instead, I tried to stiffen my spine. I was fighting the darkness—that drive toward power and greed and selfishness. There was just something about power that made one want to use it for her own gain.

Not me. I'd keep fighting it until my dying breath.

And I'd be victorious.

"You look like you're giving a graduation speech," a droll voice sounded from behind me. "So purposeful and determined."

I gasped, turning to find Lucifer leaning against the castle wall. The golden fallen angel was dressed all in black, his clothes looking like they'd cost a thousand quid, but the shadows under his eyes made him look like hell.

"What are you doing?" I demanded.

He raised a brow. "Knitting?"

I scowled. "At least make up something believable."

He shrugged, looking me up and down. "Where are you going?"

"None of your business."

"In fact, it is."

"Are you still on guard dog duty, or something?"

"Or something." He pushed himself off the wall to join me. "Well, where is it we're headed?"

"Guild City." I firmed my jaw. "And you can't stop me. Hades agreed."

He nodded, hands shoved in his pockets. He looked relaxed and dissolute, like a playboy after a long night out. But where did one *go* out in a place like hell?

"Were you watching the apothecary's cottage all night?" I demanded.

"No." His eyes flashed.

"Uh-huh. Sure."

"Whatever. Take me to your city of guilds."

"Guild City." I started toward the town. "Come on."

He followed, his long stride unhurried. I couldn't believe he was allowing me to do this, but then, it seemed Hades was capable of keeping his word. As long as he had his guard dog at my side.

Echo continued to follow my directions, leading us on a quiet route through the back of town. Lucifer looked like he was about to complain, then shut his mouth, obviously thinking better of it.

We moved down lonely cobblestone streets and passed the darkened windows of houses that might or might not be abandoned. When we reached the library, I spotted the night wolves sitting at the base of the stairs. There were nearly a dozen of them, each powerfully built with gleaming gray and black fur. Their eyes glinted with intelligence as they stared at us.

"Children of Cerberus." Wariness echoed in Lucifer's voice.

"You don't like dogs?" I frowned at him.

"'Course I like dogs. Do I look like a monster to you?"

"A pretty one, yes."

He shrugged. "Fair enough." He pointed to the dogs. "But *they* are not dogs. They are creatures of mayhem and chaos."

He wasn't wrong about that. The sight of the huge

animals sent a shiver through me. But I'd need to get past them to reach the library, so I walked slowly toward them and held my hand out flat so they could sniff me. They watched me warily.

"Hey, puppies," I said.

"Puppies?" Lucifer muttered. "Off your rocker, you are."

I shot him a glare, then looked back at the night wolves and continued to talk to them in a baby voice.

"You sound ridiculous, you know," Lucifer said.

"Yeah, yeah." Skin chilled, I knelt in front of the leader, reaching my hand out farther. I tried to use my magic the way I had before, when I'd first escaped the underworld and compelled the dogs not to attack me. I'd appealed to the light in their souls, my magic somehow connecting with theirs, and it had worked.

The massive wolf growled low, then leaned forward and sniffed my palm. He stopped growling and sat back, watching me warily. It wasn't as good as a lolling tongue and a doggier smile, but I'd take it.

"Thanks, pal." I straightened, then gestured to the stairs. "May I?"

The beast didn't move, and I took it as a yes. Quickly, I strode up the stairs. Lucifer followed, and we stopped in front of the door.

"You have a key?" Lucifer asked.

"Yep. Never let it out of my sight. Did he change the lock?"

"Not that I know of."

"Good." I dug into my pocket and removed it, then slipped it into the lock and turned it. As the lock snicked, I couldn't help but wonder where Hades was. I expected him to swoop out of the sky and stop me.

He didn't, though, and soon we were inside.

Thank fates for that.

The dark library welcomed us in, our footsteps echoing off the soaring ceiling. It sounded almost as if the library were greeting us, and the brilliant emerald and amethyst spiders all paused in their weaving to look at us.

"Hey, guys," I said.

They said nothing, of course, but returned to tending their diamond webs.

"Are you friends with all the creatures?" Lucifer asked.

"Just call me Cinderella."

"Hmm. Don't know her."

"You wouldn't."

I hurried to the portal set into the bookshelves, not hesitating now that I was inside. Quickly, I entered, letting the ether suck me in and spin me through space. I felt a tearing sensation as I left the underworld—the pomegranate potion trying to keep me there, no doubt. My stomach lurched, and my head throbbed. It spat me out in my library, and I stumbled forward, making room for Lucifer.

He exited directly behind me, looking around with curiosity. "So this is where you live?"

"Yep." Pride streaked through me. "Or at least, where I work."

"Not bad."

"Not bad?" I sputtered.

He grinned.

"You're a jerk."

He shrugged. "Where to next?"

"You can walk in Guild City? Hades can't."

"It's his curse, not mine."

"Why don't you live on earth, then? Why pick a place like the underworld?"

"I have my reasons."

"Yeah, yeah." I couldn't help but think of Alia, but I didn't ask about her. "Come on."

I led him toward the door, my insides starting to churn with the familiar pain of the pomegranate potion. I couldn't be here long, but I'd enjoy it while I could. As we left, I couldn't help but run my fingertips over the bookshelves as we passed. I missed it here. Sure, the low-profile job had been part of my plan to hide from Hades. But I'd genuinely loved it.

"You miss it here," Lucifer said as we stepped out into the watery sunlight of an overcast English day.

I shot him a glance. "You're more observant than I'd have thought."

He shrugged, then looked around, interest gleaming in his eyes. "Nice place."

I tried to see it through his eyes, through the gaze of someone who had spent a long time in the underworld. It had to be fantastic. Instead of the all-black buildings of the underworld, the white plaster and brown wood buildings were positively cheerful. The shop windows were full of color and magic, dancing teakettles and clashing swords, floating stationary and twirling dresses.

But it was the people who looked most different.

"They look so happy," Lucifer murmured, quiet enough that I knew he hadn't meant me to hear.

But I had. "There's no miserable god to drag them into his morose orbit."

Lucifer almost choked on a laugh. "Morose orbit?"

I shrugged, dodging around a gnarled old tree that grew out of the cobblestone pavement. "If the shoe fits."

"I don't think the god of death can be called morose," he said.

"I just did, didn't I?"

"He's a product of darkness. Literally. He doesn't quite have feelings like that."

Oh, he had feelings, all right. But then, Lucifer had never seen him like I'd seen him.

Lucifer continued, sounding almost like he wanted to defend his friend. "It's the nature of his soul, the darkness that formed him, that makes people feel miserable around him."

I didn't feel miserable around him. "What do you mean, the darkness that formed him. Like, literally?"

"I've said too much." He eyed a particularly nice cocktail bar to our right, one that was run by the dwarves, who were known for their restaurants. "Why don't we stop in here?"

"No. We've got places to be." I hurried past the bar, reaching the alley that led toward my guild tower.

Lucifer followed me. "What is the situation with the guilds?"

"Thirteen of them, and everyone has to be a member of one."

"Which guild is yours?"

"Shadow Guild." Most were named after the species that had started them—the witches, shifters, dwarves, or fae.

"Who's that for?"

"The weirdos."

I felt his surprise, and looked over to see his pale brows rise. "Really?"

I nodded. "The Shadow Guild is for those who don't fit anywhere else."

"I suppose there aren't a lot of goddesses running around Guild City, so it makes sense you'd be there."

"Sure." It was still hard to swallow the fact that I was a goddess.

Finally, we exited the alley onto the open square in front of the Shadow Guild tower. It rose tall in front of us, a square stone structure with ivy crawling up the sides and mullioned glass windows that gleamed dully in the pale sunlight. On the opposite side of the square from the tower sat the abandoned shops.

"Why are all the shops empty?" Lucifer asked.

I shrugged. "No one wants to own them."

"Why? You Shadow Guild people scare them off?"

"Could be, but it's probably because the tower here was hidden for a few hundred years. No tower means no reason to come to this side of town. So no businesses."

"Why was the tower hidden?"

"Oh, that's a long story. Let's just say someone didn't like the weirdos."

"Hmm."

"Sounds like you can relate."

"Maybe." He smiled, and his eyes flickered, as if concealing a hidden pain. But instead of sharing, he gestured toward the tower. "Shall we?"

"Yeah. Let's." I started toward the tower, looking forward to seeing my friends. With every step, I felt the tug of the underworld, the pain of being away. We'd need to make this quick.

I caught sight of Eve in the upper window, her pale pink hair gleaming. She leaned out and smiled. "Back so soon? Victory already?"

"I wish."

Eve frowned. "I'll come down to meet you."

I strode toward the large wooden door at the base of

the tower. It was swung open, welcoming, and I stepped through. The massive room was dominated by a huge fireplace. We'd hung art on the stone walls and outfitted it with tables and chairs to make a cozy public space for the guild.

Eve raced down the stairs to meet us, her eyebrows rising as she took in Lucifer at my side.

I knew what she was thinking—he was even hotter up close. And scarier.

"Eve, this is Lucifer. Lucifer, this is Eve."

"As in, *the*?" she asked.

He nodded. "Lovely to meet you."

She gave him a skeptical look, no sucker for pretty words, then turned to me. "What's up?"

I pulled the fabric pouch of pomegranate seeds out of my pocket and handed it to her. "This is a sample of the pomegranate tree that poisoned me. The apothecary in the underworld said they could possibly be used to find a spell that could break my curse." I looked at Lucifer. "You're not going to try to stop me, right?"

He shook his head. "My only orders are to keep you safe."

I nodded. It was as I'd expected. Lucifer was Hades' friend, not his lapdog. "Good."

Eve's brows rose, and she looked at me. "You think there might be a cure out there? I thought you searched everywhere for a cure. I tried my best, too."

"I did. And I had no luck. But I also didn't have a sample of this." I raised the seeds.

She nodded and took them from me. "I'll see what I can do."

I gripped her arms. "Thank you so much."

She looked up, a smile on her face. "Of course. I'll do anything I can to help."

Now that I'd handed off the sample, I could leave. But I really didn't want to. Not yet.

"We need to get back," Lucifer said.

I turned to him. "Spoilsport."

"Hardly." He gave Eve a significant look. "I've allowed you to come all the way to earth and try to find a way to escape Hades. I feel I've been more than accommodating."

He had been, but that didn't negate the fact that he shouldn't have that power in the first place. And my mind snagged on one specific word. "*Allow?* You *allowed* me to come here?"

He leaned casually against the stone wall and nodded. "Precisely."

"You didn't allow me to do anything. If you'll recall, one of us came out on top in our last meeting, and it wasn't you."

He rolled his eyes.

I looked at Eve. "He is such a pain in the ass."

She laughed. "I'm going to get to work on this." She

raised the bundle of seeds. "Don't want to waste any time."

"Thank you." I gave her a quick hug, then turned to Lucifer. "Okay, Satan, I have to swing by home quickly."

"*Satan.*" His brows rose. "I am *not* Satan."

I shrugged. "Six of one, half a dozen of the other. Come on, devil boy, let's go."

"I think I preferred Satan," he muttered.

"Thought you might." I said goodbye to Eve, then led him through town.

Though he wasn't as chatty as he normally was, I could see him taking in everything. For the most part, there was no expression on his face. But every now and again, he looked impressed. Maybe even a little wistful.

When we reached the ancient building that held my tiny flat, I held up my hand. "Wait down here."

"Why can't I come up?"

"Boys aren't invited."

"Ha. I'm hardly a boy."

He had that right. "Still, not invited."

"Fine." He rolled his eyes and crossed his arms, leaning against a light post. "But be back soon."

"Will do." And I meant it. Even now, my insides were turning from the pomegranate potion. It felt awful, and I knew it would only get worse.

Quickly, I let myself into the building and took the narrow stairs two at a time to my top-floor flat. The door creaked as I opened it and entered the tiny, cluttered space.

The sloped ceiling was low, but I'd hung fairy lights at the edges, giving it a homey feel. Books cluttered the shelves on the walls, and plants crowded in next to them. Mac was coming by occasionally to water them, and it heartened me to see that they looked good.

An idea popped into my head.

The underworld needed more plants.

I went from plant to plant in my flat, breaking off little sections and putting them in a small bag I found in my closet. Once I had enough clippings, I quickly changed into a new set of clothes. I was sick of the all-black wardrobe in the underworld, and an ancient, over-sized David Bowie T-shirt suited me far better. With some skinny jeans and boots, I looked like my old self.

Finally ready, I turned toward the stairs. I was heading back to hell.

9

HADES

The predawn darkness shrouded me in silence. Overhead, the sky was an inky black, and the streets were silent as I rode toward the main gate in my realm.

I'd left Seraphia alone in the bed, her small form dwarfed by the massive thing. It'd been so strangely tempting to join her—even just to sleep. Almost like softness and warmth were beckoning me.

Two things I hadn't felt before she'd arrived. Of course, I'd lain in the bed before, but I'd existed in that half world where I'd felt nothing. It was like she'd awakened something inside me.

I shoved the thought aside and rode from town, out through the main gate and down the mountain. I'd come this way with Seraphia earlier, but my destination was different this time.

Once free of the city, I nudged Horse into a gallop. He took off across the fields, tearing through the under-world, steam billowing from his nostrils. The wind tore at my cloak and hair, and I leaned low over the beast, urging him to gain more speed.

To take me away from Seraphia.

I needed to clear my head. And I needed answers that the darkness couldn't give me.

An hour later, I reached the main gate to my realm. It sat in the middle of a gnarled forest, one that was far deader than the forest Seraphia had revived. The trees rose tall and barren against a dark sky.

In the center sat a gate, a massive construction of stone and iron. Cerberus stood guard, the giant three-headed dog waiting to intercept anyone who might try to escape.

As I slowed Horse near the gate, Cerberus turned toward me. He stood as tall as a house, his fur an inky black and his three faces large and squat. His eyes narrowed at me briefly, and then his mouths opened in what I had always assumed was a canine smile. His tongues lolled out the sides, and he lowered himself to his belly.

"Hello, Cerberus."

He woofed softly, a greeting, and I rode up to him.

Even in his submissive position, he was still taller than I was while sitting on Horse.

I knew the dog wanted me to pat its head. In theory, I understood that one was meant to stroke a dog. It had never been something toward which I'd felt any inclination, however. Perhaps the faintest tug of desire, but the darkness had always risen and stomped it out.

This time, however, my palm seemed to tingle.

As I reached out to stroke one of the heads, it felt almost like an out-of-body experience. I watched my black gloved hand reach and stroke. I had no idea why I was doing this, only that there was the strongest compulsion.

Cerberus released a blissful sigh, and I frowned at him.

He liked that.

Even stranger, *I* liked that.

"Good dog." I drew my hand back and nudged Horse, moving on.

Too much of me wanted to stay with the hound, the same way I'd wanted to stay with Seraphia in the bed. What was this foreign desire for connection that was surging inside me?

I rubbed my chest, not liking the change.

As I rode through the massive gate, I could feel Cerberus's eyes on me. I didn't turn to face him, however.

The outside world beckoned to me, and I directed

Horse toward it. Outside the gates, it wasn't quite hell, nor was it quite earth. It was more of an intermediary zone—one where the humans crossed the River Styx or other gods could visit.

The river gleamed darkly in the distance, weaving slowly through the fields of gray grass. I could just barely make out the small form of Charon rowing the boat across the Styx, but I saw no one else.

With any luck, I wouldn't encounter any of the other gods. They didn't have any reason to be here, fortunately. It'd been decades since I'd seen anyone but Zeus, and that suited me. If I had my way, I wouldn't see him at all, either.

Untrue.

I did enjoy the occasional sparring match with him, as long as he wasn't putting Seraphia at risk.

I shoved away thoughts of my brother and turned away from the river. Gently, I nudged Horse and headed toward the mountain that rose high in the distance.

We reached the bottom and began to ascend. The temperature dropped with elevation, and soon, snowflakes were whipping through the dark sky. By the time we reached the summit, the snow had gathered on my cloak and sleeves, splotches of white against the dark fabric. I directed Horse toward the single tree that sat atop the peak. Like most of the trees in the underworld, it was leafless and always had been. I climbed down off of Horse, hearing snow crunch under my boot.

I approached the tree, which was sustained by the magic of the Fates. The ancient, gnarled thing was their conduit to my world.

A fierce wind whipped across my face as I stood at the base of the tree. The branches reached out to surround me in a cage of wood. Not close enough to touch, but close enough to block out the night and bind me to the tree.

Again, it reminded me of Seraphia's vines, and I felt a tug deep inside me, a memory that lit the blood in my veins and brought a wave of betrayal.

She'd done what she thought necessary, and I respected it. I respected all cunning and bravery, even when it was used against me. Still, I didn't like it.

I thrust away the thoughts and looked up at the tree. "Wise Moirai, I come to seek your wisdom."

Make your sacrifice.

The words echoed in my head.

I drew the cold air deep into my lungs and removed my gloves. Quickly, I shoved up my sleeves and drew the dagger from the sheath at my hip.

The slightest pinch of pain shot from my arm when I dragged the dagger up my wrist. I repeated the maneuver on the other arm, then lowered my arms to my sides.

Blood flowed freely, dripping to the ground and soaking the snow until it turned to dark slush. Blood loss made my thoughts go foggy and my limbs feel heavy. Though I was immortal, my blood served a purpose. If this went on too long, I would pass out, and it would take hours to recover.

But the Moirai required their sacrifice, and I required information.

I fought to stay conscious, but soon, I went to my knees, unable to stay standing. The sweet abyss of the dark called to me, beckoning me to sleep.

I ignored it, fighting to keep my eyes open.

Finally, golden magic swirled in the air, coalescing to form a young woman. She wore robes of a fine white material that was too thin to provide warmth against howling wind and snow, but warmth was the last thing she needed. She stared down at me, her dark eyes gleaming with terrible wisdom and power.

"Hades." Lachesis's voice vibrated through the night, through my body. She frowned. "You seem different."

I frowned.

"You've found her." She smiled, though it was eerie more than joyful. "Of course I can tell. There's something...complete about you."

"I've no idea what you mean."

"Hmm. She must be quite something."

"That's not the issue here."

"She's always the issue."

It was true. I'd tried to deflect, but it was true. "I'm here for information."

"Well, you've made the sacrifice. You may tell me what you require."

"I need help resisting her. Controlling her."

"Your darkness isn't helping you?"

She referred to the pit at the base of my fortress, and though it felt disloyal to confirm it, I nodded. I'd never broken away from the darkness before, never sought help elsewhere.

I hadn't even known it was possible.

But last night, while staring at Seraphia in slumber, I'd realized how weak I was becoming. I'd been willing to try anything.

"She's stronger than I thought," I said. "Her influence over me is too great."

Lachesis smiled, and once again, it was disturbing. As the king of hell, I'd seen *many* disturbing things. They didn't compete with this.

"She's susceptible to the same things you are," Lachesis said. "Physical connection. Growing to know you."

Confusion flickered. "What do you mean?"

"She must care for you in order to be willing to help you."

"Care?"

"Yes. You're familiar with the term."

In theory. Yes. In practice? No.

"You're telling me that I need to make her care for me?"

"Yes."

I'd rather she tell me to storm Mount Olympus and fight all the other gods with my bare hands.

"It won't hurt," Lachesis said. "She's already changed you. You can change her, bring her to the dark."

"She hasn't changed me." *Lie.*

It felt untrue leaving my lips.

Lachesis laughed. "You *petted* Cerberus! Of course she's changed you."

"She's *not* softened me."

"No. Nothing could do that. But a few of your harder edges have been ground down. Now all you need to do is sharpen hers. Make her care, and you'll have her on your side."

There was something in her voice... "What aren't you telling me?"

She shrugged. "You will continue to seek your greatest desire, but you may find that it changes."

"*Changes?*" The idea was surreal. I'd worked toward this for millennia. I'd been *created* for this. "It can't *change.*"

She shrugged. "We shall see." She flicked her fingertips in a dismissive gesture. "Your time is up."

Stunned, I staggered to my feet. She disappeared in a swirl of golden magic, and the tree limbs retreated, letting the cold wind roar across my face again, whipping my cloak to the side.

Change?

She said I'd already changed, and she suspected I

would change even *more*? To the point that my goal was no longer my goal?

It was absurd. Impossible to believe.

I spun to face Horse, staggering slightly from blood loss. This hadn't gone the way I'd expected. *None* of it had.

Suddenly, with Seraphia back, everything was different. Up was down and down was up, and I was meant to *change*?

It was absurd.

Even more absurd was the fact that I was supposed to make her care for me. If I wanted her help spreading the underworld to Earth, *that* was my next step?

I swung myself onto Horse's back, fighting to stay conscious. My blood would regenerate quickly, but the next thirty minutes would be difficult.

That had to be why I was finding anything credible in Lachesis's statement. It was absurd.

"To home, Horse."

The stallion headed back the way we'd come, moving swiftly down the mountain as I held on. The journey passed in a blur, my head spinning from what Lachesis had told me.

When we passed through the main gates to the city, Cerberus look at me hopefully. I clenched my jaw, riding past him.

Then I stopped.

Just because I touched the dog did not mean that I

was changing. He was simply a citizen of my domain, and I was rewarding him for his good behavior, as all proper rulers would do.

I turned back and patted Cerberus on the head, my motions stiff even to my own eyes. "Don't think this means anything."

He made a contented noise, and I moved on, riding past him. As Horse headed back toward the city, my mind raced.

I was *not* different.

Irritation pricked at me.

By the time we reached the city gate, my strength had returned. Horse galloped up the hill, reaching the gate as it opened for us. As soon as we entered, I felt it.

Seraphia.

Returned.

She must have left, as I'd given her permission to do. I'd been gone long enough that she'd have been able to get to and from Guild City.

Conflicting feelings of relief and suspicion flickered within me. Relief that she was back, suspicion as to why she'd gone.

What had she gone for?

I turned Horse toward the library, seeking Seraphia. I could sense her rough location when she was in my realm, and she was still around the large building.

Not at the front, however.

I directed Horse to the back and dismounted.

The wolves were the first sign that she was in the vicinity. They sat at the entrance to the empty garden behind the library, watching the interior.

"Move." My voice was quiet, but the wolves heard.

They parted to allow me to enter the walled-in space. It was empty save for Seraphia and Lucifer. The devil leaned against the wall, arms crossed and expression bored.

I caught his gaze and jerked my head to the exit. He nodded and left, silent as a shadow.

Seraphia had her back to me, and she knelt in the dirt, staring at something. As I watched, a plant grew in front of her, large and green.

There were more of them, I realized, tucked away. I'd had eyes only for her, so I'd missed them. But this wasn't the first one she'd planted.

She was filling my realm with life.

Something sparked inside me, something like pleasure.

As soon as I felt it, I frowned.

No.

I shouldn't enjoy things like that. I shouldn't enjoy *anything*. It distracted me from my purpose.

Anger flickered through me. Memories of Lachesis telling me I would change. That Seraphia would be the one responsible.

No. I wouldn't stand for it.

I raised a hand, directing my magic toward one of

the plants she'd put in the ground. It was twenty feet away, but my magic connected with it.

Die.

My magic wafted toward it, dark mist crawling quickly across the ground. It surrounded the plant and withered it in seconds.

Seraphia gasped and stood up, whirling around to face me. "What are you doing?"

"I didn't give you permission to alter hell."

"You've kidnapped me and want me to live here. I'm going to do whatever I want to make it habitable."

"You're planning to stay?" The most awful *hope* flickered inside my chest.

The truth flickered on her face. *No.*

"Of course you're not." I directed my magic toward another plant, killing it instantly.

"Stop!" Anger flared on her face, flushing her pale skin with pink.

Memories of her attacking Lucifer flashed in my mind. Her anger propelled her magic.

Perhaps I could accomplish two goals in one. Return hell to the way it should be and get her to advance in her magic. Her anger would make her practice, and it would be the darker side of her power that would grow. All I had to do was inflame her.

Soon, she would be strong enough to survive visiting the Place of Memories and help me seek the answers I needed.

So I killed another plant, staring at her the entire time. "Well?"

"You bastard." Her eyes flared green, so bright and fierce that she looked like the goddess I knew her to be.

She raised her hands, her magic flaring on the air. The scent of flowers and the feel of a breeze rushed over me. Her hair whipped back from her face, and her power swirled around me. There were only a few plants left in garden, but they surged to life, growing four times their size in seconds.

Their leaves grew long, the stems shooting outward toward me.

Yes.

She reached for me, directing the plants my way. I pulled back on my magic, letting them come to me. Wanting to feel them around me.

10

SERAPHIA

Rage bubbled within me, hot and fierce. Hades stood in front of me, powerful and strong in his dark armor. His hair whipped back from his face, his cloak billowing behind him.

"How dare you tear up my garden?" I demanded.

"I dare anything. I'm the king of hell."

I growled, feeding more of my magic into the plants. They grew tall and strong, their stems and leaves reaching toward Hades, wrapping around his limbs.

Yes.

Satisfaction surged inside me. My power was strong.

Dark.

I could feel it at the back of my consciousness, the

knowledge that the magic I used came from the worst parts of my soul—those that were inflamed by greed and power and strength. I sensed it all, surging through me on waves of glorious power. I'd never felt so invincible before. As if I could do anything I wanted. *Have* anything I wanted.

The vines tightened around Hades' limbs, the glossy green surfaces covering his dark armor.

He stood there, letting it happen.

A warning bell sounded from the back of my mind, so faint I almost didn't hear it.

Why was he just standing there?

I was powerful, true. But my magic was nothing compared to his.

Did he want me to be doing this?

The darkness surged inside me, the yawning hunger for power and control. It didn't care why I was doing this, just that I *was.*

Because Hades wanted me to.

He was egging me on, enraging me so that my magic would flare. The darker part of my magic.

I drew in a shuddery breath, anger surging through me.

No.

Not more anger. It would only feed the evil.

I sucked in a deep breath, trying to calm my mind, but it didn't work. The rage still bubbled inside me like a coating of oil beneath my skin.

Echo. I called on the bat with my mind, closing my eyes. I couldn't look at Hades right now. Just the sight of him pissed me off.

But Echo would help me.

Finally, I felt the faint touch of the bat on my shoulder. He weighed no more than an apple. I drew strength from him. Calm.

When I opened my eyes, the vines were receding from Hades' limbs. He frowned.

"I know what you're trying to do," I said. "I won't fall for it."

"So clever," he murmured, striding toward me. The wind whipped his cloak back, and his eyes gleamed with respect.

"Don't come any closer." I held out my hands to ward him off.

Echo launched himself off my shoulder and dive-bombed Hades, then darted away.

Hades ignored the little bat and stopped. "You're getting stronger."

I was. What had just happened…

It had felt like a tsunami of power surging through me. It'd been nearly overwhelming.

I am a goddess.

"I need to go." I hurried around him, hoping he would let me pass. My pockets were still full of sprigs I could plant elsewhere, and I'd see to it that he didn't find them. I'd seed his entire world with my power. Not just to make it beautiful, but to give myself the upper hand.

At the garden gate, I could feel the burn of his gaze at my back. I turned around, meeting his eyes.

"I'll see you tonight," he said. "And tomorrow, you'll fulfill your end of the bargain."

I swallowed hard, still having no idea how I was going to get out of that. Another problem for another time. Right now, I needed to get the hell away from him.

I hurried through the gate, passing the night wolves who lounged nearby, watching me. I ignored them. I just needed air.

Unfortunately, the underworld lacked the kind of fresh air that I wanted. But that didn't mean I couldn't find something to make myself feel better.

I raced toward the castle, knowing what I was seeking.

A library.

I just wanted to be surrounded by the calming comfort of books.

Fifteen minutes later, I'd found the perfect space. There were dozens of libraries all over the castle, and this one was situated at the back, near the ocean. The room took up the entirety of a square tower. It was only about thirty feet across, but the ceiling soared a hundred feet overhead. Bookshelves climbed all the way up the walls, surround by narrow wooden galleries accessed by even narrower stairs. On one wall, large square windows were stacked on top of each other, rising all the way to the ceiling. They were closed, but if I opened them, I knew I would hear the sea.

Echo followed me in, and I collapsed in one of the chairs, panting. There were a half dozen of them in the space, each sitting on top of the plush, beautiful rug. A fire flickered warmly in the hearth, and I stared into it.

I didn't even know what was in this library, but the subjects of the books didn't matter. With my eyes closed, I sucked in a soothing breath and let my head rest against the back of the chair.

If I pretended hard enough, I was home, in my own library. My magic was normal and fairly mundane—a bit of plant magic that I could use for healing.

It was only mundane because you avoided it.

The obnoxious voice sounded in my head, and I wanted to punch whoever said it. Unfortunately, *I* had said it. I'd had a hard enough day already. I wasn't about to punch myself in the face.

A tapping noise sounded at the window. I jerked and looked over to find a black bird fluttered at the window, trying to get me to open it.

"Beatrix!" I surged upright and raced to the window, flinging it wide. "You're here!"

She flew inside, her dark feathers gleaming in the candlelight. A moment later, she appeared in human form, her dark hair wild around her head. As usual, she wore brilliantly colored leggings and a long-sleeved top.

She always looked like she was about to go for a run, and I couldn't help but wonder if that's what she *was* going to do.

Except it wouldn't be a jog. It'd be a run from *something*. She looked like she was constantly ready to flee.

I didn't know much about her past, but she'd appeared in Guild City after being murdered, so it had to be dark.

She flung her arms around me and hugged me tight. I hugged her in turn, grateful to have her here once more.

She pulled back and looked at me. "So, you got Hades to remove my ban? I felt it when it disappeared."

I nodded, reluctantly grateful to him that he'd kept his word. Even so, I left the window open in case she wanted to make a quick getaway. "I'm so glad you could come."

She grinned. "Of course. Can't leave one of my friends stuck in the underworld without a buddy."

I laughed, then flopped into the nearest chair. "I can't tell you how good it is to see you." I shook my head. "I was just in Guild City with Eve, but as soon as I returned here, it felt like a century since I'd seen a friend."

"It's the air." She shuddered and slumped into a nearby chair. "Something weird about this place."

"You're telling me."

"How are you doing?"

I heaved a sigh, my mind racing, then decided to just tell her everything. Once I started, I couldn't shut up. It was an endless stream of babble, but Beatrix kept up, her gaze keen on me as I spoke.

Finally, I trailed off. "So it seems I'm *definitely* Persephone. I'm finally accepting it."

"But what does that mean?" she asked. "She's a goddess in all the myths, but you're only twenty-five. How does that even work?"

"I don't know!" I threw up my arms. "How could I possibly exist—a goddess who is supposedly famous—when I have no memory of that?"

She grimaced, clearly at a loss for what to say. "That's a hard one."

"No kidding. But understanding that could be the answer to controlling my magic or leaving the underworld permanently." I looked at the books around me, an idea flaring to life. I rose. "You know what? I've been totally off track."

"What do you mean?"

"I've been practicing my plant magic, trying to grow stronger, but I've been avoiding one of my key skills."

"Which is?"

"Research." I looked at the books surrounding me. "Surely there are answers somewhere." And something about this library called to me. Maybe I hadn't chosen it randomly. Maybe I'd been drawn here.

Beatrix stood. "I'll help."

"Yeah?" I smiled at her. "Thanks."

She nodded, then turned to the shelves. "Where do we start?"

"No idea. Anything you find about Persephone, I guess." I strolled to the shelves, wanting to get a feel for how it was organized. I had an affinity for books, both natural and honed over the years as a librarian. Now I was going to use it.

For the next two hours, Beatrix and I searched the shelves. There was no order that I could determine, but I'd been right that I'd been drawn here.

The shelves were full of books of ancient myths, everything that humans had ever written about the gods. I just had to find the ones about Persephone, then determine what was real and what was conjecture.

Had I lived before?

No way. I'd know if I had.

Right?

Beatrix and I searched in silence, with Echo occasionally fluttering around our heads. Every now and again, a particular book called to me. When I picked it up, I found that it was about Persephone.

Weird.

Once we finally had a stack of books, we searched together for hours with little luck, skimming the contents for any mention of reincarnation or how a twenty-five-year-old could suddenly be a goddess.

"This is not going as well as I'd hoped," I muttered.

"No kidding." Beatrix held up a book and pointed to the page. "But this one says bats are one of Persephone's sacred animals."

"Hear that, Echo?" I looked at him, but he'd had fallen asleep on a cushion, which wasn't very bat-like, if you asked me.

Suddenly, the air changed, filling with the scent of firelight. I looked up at Beatrix. "Hades."

She stood. "I'll be going, then."

I nodded. It was for the best. She was allowed here, but Hades was dangerous. He wouldn't hurt me because he needed me, but I didn't want to risk my friend. "Thanks for visiting."

"Anytime." With a flash of magic, she returned to raven form and flew through the window.

A moment later, Hades walked through the door.

He'd removed the sturdier armor he'd worn on his trip and had changed into his house armor, characterized by the thick black leather tunic. He still wore his thin black gloves, and I couldn't help but look at his hands.

He caught my gaze, and I looked away. "Didn't expect to see you so soon."

"What are you doing?"

"Trying to learn more about Persephone."

"You accept your fate?"

I just shrugged. "I want to know more about where I came from. How I exist. More about my parents."

"You never knew them?"

"No." Sadness pinged in me. "I suppose you can relate."

"Only partially. I had none in the first place, nor the desire for them."

"Oh, I had the desire for them." I looked up at the ceiling, remembered the years with Nana. She'd been the best, all the way up until she'd died. But she couldn't replace a mother and father.

Damn it, that was uncharitable. She'd been everything to me.

The memories threatened to drag me down, so I shoved them away. There was no time for such things.

He went to the window, and the breeze blew his scent over me. I resisted drawing it deeply into my lungs, though part of me wanted to. Part of me wanted to walk over to the window and wrap my arms around him.

Bad idea.

11

HADES

I looked back at Seraphia, who looked somehow...sad.

I wasn't sure if I was identifying the emotion correctly, but it seemed right.

Not liking the sight of it, I frowned. She shouldn't be sad. I wanted to make it stop, to make her feel better.

I had no idea why I suddenly had that desire, but I did.

"Have you eaten?" My tone was abrupt, and she startled, looking at me with wide eyes.

"What?"

"Food. Have you eaten?"

"Um, not lately, no."

I nodded, then sent my thoughts out into the ether.

A few moments later, food appeared on the table in the corner of the room.

"Eat." I nodded toward it.

"Um...you can't just tell me what to do."

I frowned again. This was not going how I'd expected it to. "Are you not hungry?"

"I am, but don't be so bossy."

"Bossy?" I was the king of hell, and she was calling me *bossy*.

"Yeah, bossy." She rose and strode to the table, picking up an apple and biting into it.

At least she was eating.

Taking care of people was frustrating.

This *all* was frustrating.

But I needed to persevere. Lachesis had made it clear that I needed to make her care for me. But how?

Time.

That was what had made me grow to enjoy her. Just being with her. Perhaps it would work the other way around. The mere concept sounded insane, but I had to try. She just needed to spend time with me. And if I could be reasonable—not too much of a bastard, at least —perhaps she would grow to care for me.

The concept of trying to woo her was utterly foreign. I'd never imagined that my pursuit of my goals would lead me on such a circuitous route. But then, it was meant to be a challenge, unlike simple fighting or war-making.

"Chess," I said. "Will you play me in chess?"

She looked at me, expression considering. "You really like that game, don't you?"

I nodded sharply. "I do."

But that wasn't why I wanted to play her. I couldn't care less if I played chess right now. What I wanted was more time with her, and chess could make that happen.

"Why do you like it so much?" she asked.

"Strategy. Wits. And I think you can beat me."

"You like that?"

I nodded, not having to fake it. "I do. I like that you're an equal."

She seemed to glow slightly at the words, and I realized that compliments might be a way to her heart. I should try more compliments.

Finally, she said, "I'm not sure. What's in it for me"

"Answers, if you win."

"What kind of answers?"

"What do you want to know?"

"About being a goddess. About my parents."

"I can't tell you everything you want to know because I don't know it myself. But if you win, I'll tell you what I can."

"Okay. Where do we play?"

I waved my hand, and a chess board appeared on the table in the middle of the room. It wasn't conjuring—I didn't quite have that ability—but there were a few basic life supplies that I could call upon while in my castle.

Food and chess sets were some of those things. The necessities of life.

Her eyebrows rose. "Impressive.

I nodded. "Let's play."

She took the seat across from me, and I couldn't help but look at her lips, her neck. The graceful length of her arms drew my gaze as she picked up one of her pieces.

Why was I so obsessed with her? It was unnatural.

She made her move, and I made mine. The game went quickly from there, and the minutes were some of the best I'd ever lived. In the end, she won.

A smiled flashed across her face as she leaned forward and asked, "How is it possible that I'm Persephone? She's famous and has been for thousands of years, but I wasn't alive then. Was there another version of me?"

I shook my head. "No. I've looked for you for thousands of years and never found you." They'd been long, long years, gray and dull.

"How did the myth come about, then?"

"An ancient seer once prophesied your arrival, but she did not say when it would be. The humans heard, however, and created their stories. They are famous for inventing tales to explain the world and soothe themselves."

"Fair enough. So that's how they got the name Persephone, then? And they filled in the rest from there?"

"Yes, as far as I know." I put the pieces back on the

board, enjoying the time spent sitting with her. It was oddly soothing, despite the fact that it was hard to keep my gaze from her lips. Just the sight of them made my heart race uncomfortably. I drew in an unsteady breath. "Shall we play again?"

She frowned. "I suppose. I have more questions, and I can't imagine you will answer them without incentive."

"Not if chess is an option, no."

She nodded. "Fine, then, I'll play."

The game moved quickly, and I couldn't help but admire her skill. My life would be easier if she were powerful yet pliable, but now that I'd met her, the idea of *pliable* was laughable. And anyway, I preferred the challenge. Life had become boring. Difficult, but boring.

I won the next round and carefully mulled over my questions. I had plenty of them, but it was hard to choose. Finally, I settled on what I really wanted. "Why do you live in Guild City?"

"It was safe space when my grandmother realized that I had magic that needed to be hidden."

"She knew what you were, then?"

"I don't know. But she knew I needed to be taken from Greece and protected from you."

Protected from me.

Once, that statement wouldn't have bothered me. I would have considered it entirely normal and acceptable. Now, it tugged uncomfortably at something in my soul.

A conscience? I'd read of such things, but didn't expect to have one.

"You loved her," I said.

"Of course. And she loved me."

I couldn't imagine having someone like that, but I kept it to myself.

"Another round?" she asked, clearly wanting to move the topic onward.

I nodded.

We played again, and I was so distracted by her lips that I missed a vital move. She won, and I leaned back, crossing my arms over my chest. "What will it be this time?"

She studied me. "I don't think you're all bad."

"You've told me that before." Screamed it at me, in fact, when she'd been on the verge of leaving my realm. She'd wanted me to choose the light. How little she knew if she thought that was an option. "But it's not a question."

"I suppose not." She studied me. "Why do you do this, really? There's got to be a reason."

"I was made for it."

"Made." She nodded. "Hard to imagine."

She had no idea.

"What about your scars?" she asked, and I nearly flinched.

She'd seen them, of course. While I'd been in the bath. Previously, I'd concealed them with magic. Not as a matter of vanity—I had none. It was a waste of time and none of my concern. I hid them because they revealed a weakness I didn't want anyone to know.

The fact that I was dragged back to Tartarus every millennium to be reminded of my purpose via torture was something I didn't care to share.

Yet she'd seen.

"You've already had your question," I said. "And we've time for only one more game, so let's play."

"For more questions?"

Last time we'd played, it'd ended in the most mind-altering experience of my life. That kiss on the windowsill had been the first of its kind for me, some-thing I would remember until I drew my last breath, many thousands of years into the future.

I wanted it again. The memories might be all I would have of her, and I wanted them.

"For a kiss," I said.

Her eyes widened, pupils going dark. "What?"

"You heard me." And I wanted it. More than that, I wanted her to want it as well.

"What do I get if I win?" she asked.

"Whatever you want?"

"Anything?"

"Anything at all." But she wouldn't be winning.

"All right." She put the pieces back in place, then made the first move.

I countered, and the game was on. It was fiercer than

the previous two had been, both of us determined to win. But I'd stop at nothing. I'd cheat, if necessary. The prize was too great to lose.

Finally, the game ended.

Her eyes met mine. "You won."

"I won." I stood, stepping around the table to stand by her chair.

I'd wanted this since the moment she'd returned to the underworld. Hell, from the moment she'd left.

She swallowed hard and stood.

I pulled her forward, my hands around her waist. Her scent wrapped around me, so bright and fresh that it made my head spin. She looked up at me, wide-eyed and beautiful, her skin luminous and her dark hair cascading down her back.

She looked like light and life and salvation, and I'd never wanted anything as badly as I wanted her.

With my breath caught in my throat, I bent my head to press my lips to hers. She was soft as silk, warm as fire. Everywhere her body touched mine felt like an inferno that stole my soul. For the briefest, most glorious moment, she leaned into me, pressing her body against mine. Heat exploded within me, light and pleasure.

This.

I would die for this. For her.

The mere thought shocked me so much that I pulled back.

No, that couldn't be true. How had I thought such a thing? It was the light, polluting me. It had to be. I felt it whenever I was with her like that, and it was unacceptable. Dangerous.

I retreated, my breathing uneven. I was cracking. The cold shell that kept me sane was beginning to break, and I had no idea what to do about it. "We should retire."

She just nodded, her eyes wide and her lips slightly parted. It took everything I had not to pull her into my arms again, but I couldn't. It was just too dangerous. I lost myself when I touched her like that.

I strode past her, toward the door. "Follow me."

"I'm not sleeping in your chambers."

"Yes, you are."

There was silence for a moment, and I could feel her frustration. I turned around. "Are you coming?"

She glared at me.

"Fine." I returned to her and swept her up, resisting throwing her over my shoulder. She wouldn't like that.

Instead, I cradled her against my chest, and she glared up at me. "This is weird, you know," she muttered.

"I'm not familiar with the concept."

A few moments later, we were in my quarters. I strode through the main living area into the bedroom and tossed her on the bed. She looked up at me, and for the briefest moment, I imagined myself climbing into the bed with her, touching and kissing her.

Heart thundering, I spun around and strode from the room, heading for the couch.

"This is still weird, you know," she shouted.

I didn't turn back as I said, "I will see you in the morning."

Despite the fact that I hadn't shouted, she'd heard me, and her voice drifted out from the bedroom. "Fine."

I pulled off my boots and threw myself onto the couch, not bothering to remove my clothing. It was impossible to banish her from my thoughts as I lay down, impossible not to toss and turn throughout the night.

I could think only of her, and finally, it became too much.

The tension was building to a breaking point, my confusion and frustration putting me on edge. Worse, the light was threatening. I could feel it rising within me, bringing conflicting feelings of guilt and confusion.

Was my purpose worthy? Were my goals the right ones?

I surged upright, horrified by the thought.

I didn't *question* my purpose. It wasn't how I'd been made.

Unsettled, I yanked on my boots and left my quarters.

I saw no one as I strode through the castle and

headed down the stairs to the pit at the farthest depths. It beckoned me, the darkness soothing as I stepped up to the edge and looked into the abyss. The mist rose up and soaked into me, suppressing the light, bringing relief.

I heaved a sigh, clenching my fists as I tried to get control of myself.

You are conflicted.

"I am not," I said. "I was made for this."

You were. And you will succeed.

I nodded, satisfied.

She will be ready soon. Take her to the Place of Memories. Learn the location of doomsday and fulfill your destiny.

The words filled me with purpose, and I breathed deeply, wanting to be satisfied. Wanting to feel whole and committed again.

But I didn't. Not entirely.

Under normal circumstances, a visit to the abyss might be enough. Not this time. Though I stared into it, I didn't feel completely normal. Almost as if Seraphia were changing my very makeup.

The idea was terrifying.

I turned from the pit and headed for the door that opened to the sea. Though the castle itself was situated on a cliff overlooking the water, the chamber at the base of the building was closer to sea level. A small door at the back led directly out to the ocean.

At the door, I shucked off my clothes, retaining only

the dark shorts I wore underneath. I reached for the door and pulled it open, the iron hinges shrieking, having long ago gone rusty from the salt air. Outside, the sea roared. The door was set into the side of the cliff, and the waves were pitch black as they crashed against the stone wall below me.

I dove off, letting the coldness envelop me.

Physical exertion to the point of near-death was the closest thing I could get to an escape. I welcomed it, cutting through the salty water, letting the waves wash over my skin.

Soon, my mind calmed, and my body turned to the task of moving ever onward.

12

*S*ERAPHIA

It was dark when I woke, the room strangely empty. I was still in Hades' bed, but he was gone. Not that he'd ever been in the bed, but I was certain he was no longer on the couch.

"Hades?" I called, just to check.

No answer.

But it was the middle of the night. Where the hell *had* he gone?

I climbed out of bed, too curious to resist. Quickly, I pulled on my jeans and boots, then crept out into the main sitting room. As expected, the couch was empty.

The hallway outside was silent, and the quiet felt still as the grave. But I could almost sense him, like a pulling sensation. I followed it, creeping through the halls. The lamps along the walls had been dimmed, casting deep shadows in front of me.

I moved silently, drawn to the bottom floor of the castle, toward a hallway that was more austere than the others I'd seen. Was I returning to the dungeons?

No, not quite.

A huge wooden door loomed in front of me, a dark mist hovering near the floor in front of it.

Hades?

Skin chilled, I walked toward the door. The large iron handle was smooth beneath my hand as I pulled it open, and the door swung silently on its hinges, revealing a wide staircase that spiraled into the depths of the castle.

I stared hard into the darkness, my bones gone cold with fear.

Hades is down there.

Did he need my help? Not bloody likely.

But what *was* that place?

There were answers there. They called to me, a siren song impossible to resist.

I took the stairs two at a time, squinting into the dark. When I reached the enormous chamber at the bottom, I gasped and stumbled backward.

The ceiling soared overhead, rough stone that appeared carved out by hand. Or by dark magic. I could feel it so strongly that it turned my insides.

The power wafted from the middle of the room, calling to me. As much as it made me feel ill, I was drawn to it. Slowly, I started forward, realizing that the magic came from a wide, dark pit that plunged far into the earth.

Its pull was so strong that an army couldn't have stopped me from moving toward it. Reaching inside me, it gripped a hand around my heart and dragging me closer.

Heart pounding, I reached the edge of the pit. I stared down into the depths, finding actual *stars*. They glinted bright white, and it was like looking up into the heavens.

Just like looking into the sky, there was a sense of infinite possibility. Of purpose. My terror transformed into understanding.

Look deeper.

The voice echoed in my head, feeling like it was part of me.

I obeyed, helpless to resist. As I squinted into the darkness, I began to see visions. They were shadowy at first but gradually coalesced to become more solid.

A black mist swirled, twisting and turning about itself as it grew thicker and thicker. Soon, it was so dense that it looked solid, until finally, Hades stood before me, perfect and whole.

I blinked, shocked.

He wasn't here—it was just a vision—but had I just witnessed his creation?

He truly *was* formed of the darkness. In the most literal sense.

How had I felt any light in him at all, then? Surely that should be impossible.

But I'd *felt* it.

As I watched the image of him, I could feel his conflict. It was almost like we were one and the same. There *was* light in him, but it fought against the darkness. I could feel his pain as if it were my own, and it felt like my soul was being pulled out through my navel.

I staggered and went to my knees, barely able to keep myself upright. The conflict was tearing through me, and I wrapped my arms around myself, trying to keep from shattering.

The stone bit into my knees where I knelt right at the edge of the abyss. I couldn't look away from where the stars spun through the blackness. A dark mist wafted from the depths, curling up through me and soothing the agony.

I leaned into it, shuddering as it drove away the pain.

The darkness calmed the horrible torment caused by the light, and the farther I leaned into it, the better I felt. I leaned so far over the pit that I lost my balance and fell, plummeting into the depths.

A scream tore from my throat as the wind whipped my

hair back from my face. I scrabbled to catch something, my arms pinwheeling. Fear blanked out my thoughts as I tried to stop my fall, but there was nothing I could do.

Strong arms plucked me out of the air and yanked me toward a strong chest, cradling me close. My descent stopped abruptly. The scent of firelight surrounded me, and I knew.

Hades.

He'd caught me.

I gasped, clinging to him, as he shot out of the abyss, flying upward so fast that my stomach dropped. He slowed abruptly, coming to land on the stone platform outside of the pit. The cavern soared around us, dark and ominous, but I could only focus on him.

Panting, I didn't let go of his neck.

He didn't let go of me, either.

For some reason, he was mostly naked, his skin cold. His hair was damp around his face, and he looked at me with such fear in his eyes that I almost couldn't believe it.

"Why did you do that?" His voice was rough. "To enter the pit is death. You could have killed yourself."

"I didn't mean to." I blinked, suddenly realizing. "You risked death by coming after me?"

He grunted, then set me down but kept a grip on my arms as I staggered. Even when I'd righted myself, he didn't let go.

"I saw you born," I said, my head still spinning.

"Created."

"Created, yes." I nodded. That was definitely the word for it. "The darkness felt so good. It was amazing."

He made a low noise in his throat, as if unsure of how to respond.

"Is that was it feels like for you?" I prodded.

He hesitated before speaking. "Not amazing, no. The only thing that feels amazing is..."

"What? What were you going to say?"

"You."

I swallowed hard, unable to believe it. "The darkness really doesn't feel good to you?"

"It feels like...nothing. Like the pain goes, and I am left with nothing."

Left with nothing.

It sounded awful, but compared to the pain I'd felt, it was probably pretty good.

I remembered now, feeling the light inside him. It had fought to come to the surface, fought so hard it had hurt. It had torn me apart inside. I gasped at the memory, clutching my stomach. The only thing that had made me feel better was leaning into the darkness, embracing it. "You've already fallen to the dark."

"There was nothing to fall to. I was made of it."

"It can't be the only way."

"It *is*." His hands tightened on my arms, but not painfully. "I owe it everything."

I looked up at him, desperate. "You don't owe it anything. It keeps you here, bound. Alone."

"I'm not alone."

Hades

I stared down at Seraphia.

Alone.

She thought I was alone.

And maybe I had been. But with her here, it was like those long years had never existed. Like she'd opened a window and let in the light. Just being with her filled me with such a warmth and joy that it made my head spin.

She looked up at me with such...*emotion* in her eyes. I couldn't identify it all, but there was something compelling about it. Something good.

It was the strangest feeling, but I liked it. She changed everything just by being here.

And she'd almost died. I'd finished my swim and walked back into the room right as she'd fallen into the pit. The memory still made fear lance through me, sharp and pure.

I'd almost lost her.

A world without Seraphia was no world at all.

I realized, for the briefest moment, that I wasn't

thinking of my end goal or why I needed her. I was thinking just of her. Of how I wanted to spend every moment with her. And I'd almost lost that.

The urge to be close to her—to kiss her—grew so strong that I couldn't resist. Whatever concerns I'd had before, whatever I'd been trying to avoid, didn't matter in the face of all this. My resistance stood no chance in the face of her.

I bent my head and captured her lips with my own.

She made a startled sound of pleasure, then wrapped her arms around my neck and kissed me like the world was ending. She tasted so sweet that I could have forgone food for eternity if I could kiss her instead.

I wrapped my arms around her waist and pulled her to me, leaning into the feel of her. She was so slight yet strong, and I reveled in the soft curves of her form.

She plunged her hands into my hair, and I groaned, wanting more of her. Wanting to lay her down and feast on her. She tasted divine, all sweetness and light. I couldn't get enough of her as I devoured her mouth, holding her tight against me.

When the voice of the darkness whispered inside my head, I was almost able to ignore it.

You are fracturing.

I didn't care.

But Seraphia seemed to hear as well.

She jerked back, eyes wide. "What was that?"

Breathing hard, I stared down at her. It took a few moments for my mind to return to sanity.

The darkness had spoken.

Near her.

Fear shot through me. I didn't want it near her.

She looked toward the pit, her eyes widening. "Is someone in there?"

Was there? I honestly did not know. I'd always thought the voice was something like a god, yet greater than me or Zeus or Poseidon. The voice of the universe speaking directly to me.

But what if it had form?

Could it hurt Seraphia?

The thought tore me apart. I'd been loyal to the darkness my entire life, yet now I questioned it? How was that possible?

Seraphia.

I gripped her arm. "Come. We must go. It's not safe here."

"But it's in your castle."

I turned to her, knowing my eyes blazed with hellfire. *"I'm* not safe."

Something flashed in her gaze, and her jaw hardened. All the softness was wiped from her face. "You're right."

She strode past me, away from the pit and the danger that I brought to her life. I watched her go, then followed, unable to face the darkness and what it had said.

Fracturing.

Was I really?

Was she?

13

SERAPHIA

I'd stormed back to bed after leaving Hades. When morning came, he was nowhere to be found—typical. As I didn't sense immediate danger, however, I allowed myself to sit up and rub my face as I eased back into consciousness.

Last night.

Holy fates, last night.

Two kisses. Not one, but two. Like we were normal people getting to know each other. Falling for each other.

It was too insane to be believed.

No. I didn't have to believe it, actually. Sure, it had happened. But it was just physical. It didn't have to mean anything. I wouldn't let it.

A faint squeaking noise sounded from the window, and I looked over to see Echo.

Was he *laughing?*

"Can you read my thoughts?" I demanded.

He nodded his little head.

I threw a pillow at him, and he launched himself into the air, swooping though the room.

"I'm in control, Echo. I'm not going to let Hades sway me."

He made a noise that I was certain meant *suuure.*

"You little rat," I said, then grinned at him, unable to help myself. "Cute rat, though."

He landed on my shoulder, and I walked toward the main living area. I knew Hades was gone before I even looked, and I wasn't surprised to find a tray of breakfast sitting on the table. It was becoming routine to wake alone with breakfast waiting.

I stared at it, debating.

Today, we were meant to begin looking for whatever it was he sought. Was I going to help him with that? It had to be bad, whatever he wanted.

He wants to destroy the world.

Memories flared in my mind, so bright and bold that they overtook my vision. It was almost like I was at the Temple of Shadows again, watching my future self walk alongside Hades. In that vision, we'd been on earth. He'd accompanied me, and I'd knelt in a field, touching the waving grass and sucking the life from the earth.

He wanted to spread the dominion of hell, over-taking everything warm and good about my home. Spreading more of the darkness that had frozen his own realm.

It had created him. I'd seen it myself.

How had he survived so long here? I'd felt what it was like to be him, and it was terrible. But I'd also felt the good inside him. He was only doing what he'd been created to do, and I'd *felt* the part of him that fought it. He didn't really want to do it, did he?

Another memory crept into my mind.

You are fracturing.

The darkness within the pit had spoken to us. To him? To me?

I shivered.

I *was* fracturing. Feeling the dark magic rise inside me, succumbing to Hades. Without a doubt, that darkness was talking to me. But it had to be talking to him as well. He kept moving toward the light, only to turn away.

What if I could help him? Save him, even?

Maybe that was my role?

I chewed on my lip, mind spinning.

It wasn't like I had any other options while I was here, anyway. Eve was still working on a potion to help break the pomegranate curse, and I needed to master my magic if I didn't want the darkness to overtake me. I hadn't finished that yet.

Anyway, in the vision, I had to *willingly* go to earth with Hades and help spread the darkness. I just wouldn't do it. I'd uphold my part of the bargain and go with him today to find the information he sought. If I could, I'd try to find a way to turn him to the side of the light.

Decided, I grabbed a pastry and went to the bathing room. I desperately needed a bath, and then I would find Hades.

I ate the pastry quickly, then slipped off my clothes and walked into the warm, steaming water. It glittered crystal clear, and I felt the magic within it. Hopefully, that magic kept it clean; otherwise, I was using a swimming pool as a bath, and that was *really* iffy.

Reluctantly, I made quick work of bathing even though I wanted to linger, then went to the living room to check out the clothes I'd seen draped over a chair in the main quarters. He must have had Kerala deliver them.

He was considerate, given that he was the king of hell. I'd have thought these little things would escape him, but they didn't.

I took some of the clothes—underthings and trousers—but put on the David Bowie shirt I'd changed into yesterday in my flat. It was clean enough, and I wanted the reminder of who I really was. I should have packed a bag of clothes, now that I thought of it. I'd been so obsessed with my plants, though. At least I'd planted most of them before Hades had shown up. He'd never be able to find them all.

Once I was dressed, I left the room to find Hades. Something told me he would be waiting for me on the front steps of the castle, so I hurried in that direction. When I stepped out into the miserable gray light of morning, it seemed like the sky was slightly brighter than it ever had been. Still dark and dreary, but maybe not quite so miserable.

My attention was caught by Hades, who stood waiting by Horse.

How had I known he'd be there? Were we more connected than I thought?

He was dressed in the dark, heavy armor that he wore when we left the city, and he looked like he was ready to ride into battle. He was terrifying in a way that made my heart race, but it wasn't all fear.

"Are you ready to go?" he asked.

I nodded and descended the stairs toward him. "Where are we going?"

"Kamarina, in Sicily."

"On earth? I thought you couldn't walk upon the earth."

"I can't. At least, not freely. There are parts I am able to visit, such as your library, but special rules surround those places."

"Why Kamarina, then?"

"It is a territory of the gods. There is an ancient temple there, built for the Oracle of Kamarina. It is imbued with our magic, and therefore, I can walk upon that ground."

"All right." I looked for Sally. "I want my horse, though."

For a split second, he looked as though he might argue. Then he nodded, his gaze flicking to a servant who stood at the far end of the stairs. The servant nodded and hurried off.

Once we were alone, tension tightened the air between us. Memories of last night flashed in my mind, and I found I couldn't bear it any longer. I looked at him, meeting his dark gaze. "It meant nothing, and it won't happen again."

Something flickered in his eyes, unidentifiable... unless I was willing to acknowledge that it might have been hurt.

But no way.

I couldn't possible hurt Hades. He had no feelings.

He jerked his head in agreement, then stepped around me. I turned to watch him approach the servant who brought Sally. He took the horse's reins, and the servant disappeared toward his post at the end of the stairs. When Hades turned back to me, his face was impassive.

I strode to him and stopped next to Sally's saddle,

gripping it with my hands and raising my foot into the stirrup. Out of the corner of my eye, I caught sight of Hades lifting his hands to help me get onto my mount.

"I can do it." My voice was too sharp. Too harsh.

He disappeared from behind me, striding toward Horse.

Damn it. I hadn't meant to sound like such a bitch. I shouldn't care, considering that he'd kidnapped me. But still, after what I'd seen last night, I kind of did. I was just having a hell of a time processing what was happening between us.

We were *enemies*.

So why did it feel less so every minute?

I should hate him for what he'd done to me. And I did. At least, part of me did.

Whatever.

I shook my head, driving the thoughts from my mind. I still stood on the castle steps, and I used the added height to clumsily mount Sally, barely managing to swing my leg over the saddle. I reached for her reins and gripped them in a way that mimicked Hades. "Please don't kill me, Sally," I whispered. "Just go nice and easy."

She made a whinnying noise and shifted abruptly. I nearly lost my seat, and Hades' voice cut through the air, commanding. "Styx."

Immediately, Sally settled down.

I looked at him. "You named her after the river of the dead?"

"What else would I call her?"

"Horse Two? Horse the Second?"

He nodded. "Not a terrible idea. Now come."

He nudged Horse with his heels and turned the beast toward town. I followed—or rather, Sally did. I just held on.

"I'm not calling you Styx," I said. "Sally is much nicer."

"And ridiculous," Hades said.

"I like it." But I couldn't help the small smile that tugged at the corner of my lips. It *was* ridiculous. And that was part of the charm. I joined him at his side, my mount a few feet from his. "How do we get to Kamarina? Is there a portal at the library?"

"No, it's on the outside of my territory, through the gate that Cerberus guards."

Excitement and fear thrummed within me, a heady cocktail. "I'm going to get to meet Cerberus?"

He shot me a perplexed look, his brow slightly creased. "You're...looking forward to that?"

"He's the most famous dog ever, so yes."

"Fond of dogs, aren't you?"

"Who isn't?" My brows shot up. "Do *you* not like dogs?"

"You sound as if you are accusing me of flaying people alive. Which I also do, by the way." He shook his head. "I should remind you that I don't like *anything*, Seraphia. I don't even understand the concept."

"Hmm." He said that, and I could tell he partially believed it. But he'd sure seemed to like me last night.

I kept that tidbit to myself, though, as we rode in silence through the town. As usual, his crown appeared on his head, and his subjects streamed outside, their gazes full of awe as they looked at us. Nothing had ever made me want to return to the quiet of my library so much as the weight of their heavy stares.

I shook the thought away. If I wanted to survive this, I needed to focus on the present, not on fantasies of disappearing back into my quiet library where nothing ever bothered me.

Hades led me through town and out the gate. Horse and Sally picked up the pace until they were galloping, and I held on tightly, thighs burning. To my left, the cliffs plunged down into the dark sea. I could hear the waves crashing and smell the salt air, but we veered away and headed through the fields.

We rode toward the forest that I'd revived, and I couldn't help but look at my creation. It was so far in the distance that I couldn't see it very well, but I could feel the life flowing from it. As we neared, I was able to make out the dark green leaves of the trees. They looked healthy, though not particularly bright. It wasn't like I was down here spreading a cheerful version of life like a fairytale princess, but it was nice to see the place looking better.

"This way." Hades' voice carried over the wind, and he directed Horse away from the forest.

Reluctantly, I followed, and soon, we were deep in another forest. The ancient oaks were twisted and gnarled, their limbs as leafless as the other forest had once been. I could feel life lurking in the underbrush, small animals and insects. A few birds flitted through the branches, though they were so fast I never got a good look at them.

My palms itched to help this place, to give it back some life so it could flourish. I'd do it differently than last time, however. No way I wanted to get into the habit of strangling bunnies.

"We don't have time," Hades said.

Shocked, I looked at him. "Can *you* read my mind?"

It would just be too much if both he and Echo could. Fear chilled my spine.

"No. But it is obvious what you are thinking. You want to help."

"Hmm." I stared at him, searching his expression until I was finally satisfied that he was telling the truth.

Our horses slowed as the trees grew closer together, until finally, I started to feel something odd in the air. It was a life force, but enormous. Whatever we were approaching was huge.

I shivered. My magic was getting crazy strong, if I could sense something like that.

"What's up ahead?" I asked, my voice quiet.

"Cerberus."

Cerberus.

I strained to see through the trees, finally spotting a massive, dark shape. As we neared, I caught sight of a tall stone and iron gate. Two sconces glowed with orange light, and leafless, gnarled oaks grew around it, making it look like the realm Halloween forgot. Cerberus sat near it, the enormous black dog resting on his haunches as he stared at us with all three sets of eyes.

As soon as Cerberus saw Hades, his three mouths opened in a doggy grin, and his tongues lolled.

Fear collided with the sensation of *oh, my fates, he's cute*, and it was the weirdest damned thing. I didn't know if I wanted to run screaming or hug him.

When he lowered himself to his belly and stared longingly at Hades, my heart lurched.

Oh, my God, I want to hug him.

We rode past, Hades insistently putting his mount between me and Cerberus. I watched as Cerberus inched his head toward Hades, and the god's brow creased. After a long moment of debate, he reached out and awkwardly patted one of Cerberus's heads.

The beast made a long, low sound of delight, and Hades nodded stiffly at him.

I grinned widely, unable to help myself.

Hades caught me looking and frowned. "Do not think that I make a habit of such things."

"Of course not." But my grin still stretched at my cheeks, and I vowed that if I got a chance, I was coming back here to pet Cerberus myself.

But even more exciting than Cerberus—if such a thing were possible—was the fact that Hades had freaking *petted* him. He'd done it like a robot learning to feel, or perhaps mimicking humans, but he'd *done it.*

He was definitely fracturing.

As we passed Cerberus, Echo appeared. He flitted back to sit on one of Cerberus's heads, and it seemed like they might actually be friends.

We were nearly to the massive gate when Hades spoke. "Be alert. Though the land outside these gates is closest to my realm, it is not fully my dominion. It is a halfway point between the underworld and the realms beyond, and the other gods have an easier time walking upon this land."

I nodded. "All right."

Hades directed Horse through the gates, and I followed.

Almost immediately, I spotted the river in the distance. It gleamed darkly as it snaked through the fields. A small boat crossed it, carrying a tall man in a dark cloak.

Charon.

Holy fates, this was wild.

"There's no one in Charon's boat," I said.

"There rarely is these days," Hades said. "Afterworlds are populated by those who believe in them. Very few people worship the ancient Greek gods anymore."

"Does that bother you?" I studied his face, getting the distinct impression that it did not.

"No. I prefer it."

"Too much work?"

He shrugged. "I do what I must, but I find no joy in ruling the dead."

"You find joy in nothing." Nothing except me.

He nodded. "Come. We are nearly there."

He turned Horse to the left, approaching a small copse of dead trees outside the massive stone wall that surrounded the underworld. In the distance, a mountain loomed. I shivered, grateful we weren't climbing to the top of it.

Once we were inside the copse, Hades dismounted, then came to help me down. I wanted to protest, but the memory of nearly falling on my arse last time I'd tried this was impossible to forget.

"Thanks." My voice was stiff as he gripped my waist, his touch sending a shiver through me.

As soon as he set me down, I backed up.

His lips thinned just slightly before he said, "Come. The portal is this way."

14

HADES

Seraphia and I approached a shimmering patch of air that marked the portal. At the entrance, I held out my hand to her. It wasn't entirely necessary that we stay connected while traveling through the portal, but it was safer.

She looked at it skeptically for the briefest moment, then reached out and grasped me.

Warmth shot up my arm. Though I tried to suppress any enjoyment, it was impossible. Touching her quieted my soul in the same way that the darkness did. I drew in a ragged breath, shoving away the thought.

"Come." I stepped toward the portal, and she followed.

As the ether sucked us in and spun us through space, I held tight to her hand. A moment later, it spat us out on a rocky cliff. The sea crashed below, the waves roaring as the scent of salt filled the air. Behind us, the ruins of the ancient Greek city crouched against the hills that rose up from the cliff.

For the briefest moment—not even a second—the day was bright. Then, as if responding to my mere presence, thick clouds rushed over the sun, shrouding us in near-darkness.

"Holy fates." Seraphia stumbled, and I righted her, wrapping my arm around her waist and gripping her to me.

I wanted to hold onto her like this forever, but she pulled away.

"What just happened with those clouds?" she asked, her face turned toward the sky.

"It's me."

"Are you like a vampire and can't go into the sun?"

I shook my head. "No. It's just the response of the sun, to hide from me."

"That's...unexpected." She looked me up and down, the slightest bit of fear glinting in her eyes. "I didn't know the sun was afraid of anything."

"I'm not sure I would call it fear." More like a curse.

A curse? I'd never thought of it that way before. It was just the nature of things, that darkness would follow me always. Why was I suddenly thinking this way?

I shook the troubling notion away and looked at her. "It's just the way it is."

"Hmm."

It was clear that a hundred thoughts were flashing through her mind, but she didn't speak them. Instead, she turned and inspected our surroundings. I followed her gaze, taking in the bleached ruins of the town that had once existed here. The buildings had been demolished by time, and their remains crumbled around us with sparse, tough grass growing up between them. As I watched, they began to reconstruct themselves, the whitewashed walls and terracotta roofs reappearing. Tiny windows looked like eyes into the houses, and little gardens sprouted out front. The paths cleared, as if people had trod over them for hundreds of years.

"What's happening?" Seraphia asked.

"When a god walks upon the earth in a place that once worshiped him, it returns to its former glory."

Her eyes widened as she took it all in. "Will the people appear?"

"No. They are gone."

"In the underworld?"

"Among other places."

The city had fully reformed now, the buildings lining the streets and the fountains shooting water. In the distance, a large temple speared toward the cloudy sky, sitting at the edge of a rocky promontory that jutted out over the water. A narrow land bridge connected the city to the temple, and the gray waves crashed on either side of it.

I pointed to the temple. "Come. That is where we will meet the Oracle."

Her gaze flashed to me. "What will you ask her?"

"Not me, you."

"Me?"

I nodded. "Ask her about your family. Your past."

She frowned. "Wait, what? How does this have anything to do with advancing your goal?"

I frowned, unsure of how to answer. She'd wanted answers last night, so I'd brought her here. I hadn't thought much more than that.

Her eyes widened. "Holy fates, it doesn't." She narrowed her eyes at me. "Did you bring me here to be *nice*?"

"No." I nearly laughed, but my throat was too rusty from disuse. "That is not something that I am."

"No. You're not nice." She shook her head. "That is a weak, silly word. But this is kind."

I frowned, uncomfortable with that word as well. "Just go ask your questions. I cannot promise that you will find anything."

She nodded, and after one lingering look at me, she started down the path by the sea. I followed her, staying close behind.

The path cut along the cliff, which rose fifty feet

above the crashing waves below. She stared down at them, a wistful look on her face.

"This is similar to where I spent my earliest years, on Cyprus." She looked back at me. "Until we had to leave."

"Because of me."

She nodded, her gaze shadowed.

Something sharp slipped between my ribs, a blade honed of guilt.

I swallowed hard. Guilt? Why should I possibly feel guilt?

Gods, feelings were miserable things.

"It's strange that you should have dominated so much of my childhood—all of the running and hiding —and yet, now that I'm with you, you're not nearly as bad as I thought."

For the briefest moment, something bright shone in my heart. Happiness, perhaps. Or hope?

It was followed immediately by an immense wave of self-disgust. She couldn't think that of me. It was too dangerous.

I gripped her arm and jerked her to me. She gasped, stumbling until she righted herself with a hand against my chest. Wide-eyed, she looked up at me. "What the hell is your problem?"

"*Don't* think that I am kind, for I am not. I *will* disappoint you."

She scowled at me. "Oh, I know it. Silly me to have forgotten."

Somehow, the damned knife returned between my ribs. I let go of her and stepped back, then nodded toward the path that led to the temple. "Go on."

She spun on her heel and stalked off.

I drew in a deep breath and followed, my gaze riveted by her form. The temple sat alone on a thin peninsula that jutted into the sea. The path to access it was narrow, and the cliff walls dropped sharply into the gray-blue ocean that crashed against the stones below.

We reached the temple steps a few minutes later. The temple was circular in construction, similar to the Temple of Shadow. Unlike that one, however, this temple had solid walls of white marble.

"I will wait for you here," I said. As much as I wanted to accompany her in, she needed to be able to ask the questions she wanted. My presence might deter that. Anyway, I needed to keep watch. We were no longer within the protection of my realm, and the other gods might sense that. They had no desire for me to complete my fated task and would take any opportunity to stop me.

Including killing Seraphia.

She didn't look at me as she nodded and raced up the stairs, entering the temple silently. I turned away and inspected my surroundings.

The city was ghostly quiet, the buildings forming silent sentinels from the past.

When the air sparked with magic, I stiffened. It

swirled with golden sparks, and I frowned. "Who's there?"

In front of me, the air solidified to form the shape of a woman. She was slender and ancient, yet timeless, her eyes blue and bright. Beautiful. Despite her age, she was as regal as a queen, and power emanated from her like perfume. The white robes that draped her form were shot through with gold and decorated with blue gems that glittered like her eyes.

"Oracle?" I frowned at her. "Why are you here? Shouldn't you be inside?"

"This is all my domain." She gestured to it. "And you are the one that I would like to speak to."

"There is someone inside waiting for you."

"Yes, I know. And I will go there soon." Her gaze traveled up and down my form. "My, my, Hades, how you have changed."

"I have not." My voice was too stiff even to my own ears.

She laughed. "I have seen all for millennia, and I see you, my dear boy."

Dear boy?

I blinked at her. "The Oracle of Kamarina is known for being terrifying."

She shrugged a shoulder. "And I am, to some. But what is the point when I am facing the king of hell? I cannot frighten you, so I will not try."

"What do you want with me?"

"A message." She gestured to the temple. "Within those walls stands the other half of you."

"Other half? What do you mean?"

"Light and dark, you are each half of a whole, incomplete without the other."

"I am complete."

She shrugged. "Perhaps you feel that way, but that does not negate the truth of your magic. You each need the other to complete your goals. You will save each other."

Understanding dawned. "She will be my queen."

"That is not what I meant. But yes, that is fated."

"She won't like the sound of that."

"Then you will have to convince her."

"How do I do that?"

"I'm not here to give you all the answers. But remember this—your power is not complete without her, nor hers without you. The only way forward is together."

With that, she disappeared.

I heaved a sigh and dragged my hand over my face.

Fate save me from oracles.

"Brother." The voice echoed with power as it traveled across the waves, and I looked up.

There, rising from the sea, stood Poseidon. His armor glinted a silvery blue, as if it were made from water itself. Unlike Zeus, who embraced modern life,

Poseidon was more like me. He stayed in his realm, except for brief visits like this.

I drew my bident from the ether, the bi-pronged staff familiar in my hand. "We are not brothers."

In return, Poseidon drew his trident. "Why are you here, Hades?"

"That is none of your concern."

But Poseidon wouldn't consider that true. He'd want to take this opportunity to stop me, the same way Zeus had. I resisted shooting a glance toward the temple. If he didn't know that Seraphia was here, I did not want to alert him. She needed time with the Oracle, and I'd prefer to get rid of Poseidon myself.

"Of course it is." He smiled and raised his trident, and I braced myself for battle.

15

SERAPHIA

"Hello?" My voice echoed as I spun in a circle, inspecting the empty temple around me.

The massive room was round, and tall pillars encircled me, supporting the domed ceiling. Beneath my feet, the mosaic was a gorgeous design of glittering stones laid out in a starburst pattern.

There was something oddly familiar about this place.

A sense of power sparked on the air behind me, and I whirled around, spotting a woman as she appeared at the edge of the tunnel.

I frowned, shock racing through me. "*Nana?*"

Nana smiled, her wrinkled face so beloved and

familiar, despite the fact that I hadn't seen her since her death years before.

"Seraphia." She held out her arms, which were draped in gorgeous white fabric, shot through with gold thread and studded with blue gems.

I ran to her, just barely managing to not throw myself into her arms. She was so slight that I didn't want to crush her. She hugged me hard, her arms far stronger than I remembered them being.

I pulled back and looked at her, taking in her bright blue eyes and halo of gleaming white hair. "What are you doing here?"

"The question is, what are you?"

I scowled at her. "Don't talk in riddles. You and I both know you are supposed to be dead, and yet you're here, looking like a high fashion version of a Greek goddess."

"An oracle, dear."

My jaw dropped. "*You're* the Oracle of Kamarina?" She shrugged one shoulder, and I just stared at her. "No way."

"Way."

I laughed, overjoyed despite my confusion. If I were an idiot, I'd be annoyed that she hadn't told me. Instead, my beloved grandmother was back with me. I didn't care what secrets she'd kept. "What's going on? You've always been an oracle?"

"I have." She nodded. "I was never supposed to tell

you, though, or fate would not have worked the way it was meant to."

My head reeled. "So I'm supposed to be trapped in the underworld?"

"Trapped is quite a relative term, if you want to be somewhere."

"Of course I don't want to be in the underworld."

"Don't you?" Her gaze flicked to the door. "Your Hades is quite attractive."

"And evil." I raised my brows at her. "Don't be shallow."

She laughed. "There's much you do not know yet, but you will. In time."

"What can you tell me?"

"You are truly Persephone, so get any doubt out of your head right now."

"I've accepted that. What of my parents?"

"That is something you must learn on your own. But I can tell you that you have never lived before. There was no version of Persephone before you, just the myths that were based in little more than human fantasy."

I nodded. "Okay, that's a relief, actually. Hades said the same, but I'm glad you're confirming it."

Nana squeezed my arms, her gaze turning intense. "But it's important that you go with Hades to the place that he seeks. Only there can you prove yourself and calm the darkness within you."

Shock ricocheted through me. "What?"

"You are fighting to learn to control your power, are you not? To master it so that you don't fall prey to the darkness that wants to compel you?"

"Yes, exactly. So that I can *avoid* going with Hades to bring about the apocalypse."

"That is the difficult part, my dear. To defeat what you fear most, you must face it. If you do not, the darkness will overwhelm you. You must prove yourself against it, or you will fall to it."

"So I have to go with him to the location and *not* destroy the earth?"

She nodded. "It is fated. What happens there must come to pass. It is the only way to save your own soul. And to save his."

Hope flared within me. "*Can* he be saved?"

She nodded. "It will not be easy, and it will not take the path you expect. But yes, if you are brave enough and strong enough, it can be done."

Brave enough and strong enough.

That felt like a tall order.

From outside, something loud crashed. It was followed by a bellow, and my gaze flicked to Nana's. "What's that?"

"A fight." She frowned. "Poseidon has found you. It is time to go."

"No!" I gripped her arms. "When will I see you again?"

"You may return when you wish."

There was another crash, and I flinched. But I couldn't go yet, not until I knew she wouldn't disappear for good. "You'll be here? You promise?"

She smiled. "I promise." She hugged me tightly, the most divine thing in the world, and then she pushed me back. "Now go. The gods are immortal, but not against each other."

Fear sliced through me, and I nodded. I gave her one last look, memorizing her beloved face, then sprinted from the temple.

Outside, the scene was chaos.

Hades stood on the temple steps with his back to me, his cloak billowing in the gale. He gripped his bident in one hand and raised the other, his magic surging on the air. The scent of fire was so strong, I could have sworn there was a blaze somewhere nearby. Rocks rose up in front of Hades, levitating to form a wall between him and Poseidon.

The other god stood upon an enormous wave, his armor glinting like water. He clutched a trident in his hand, the prongs spearing at the sky. He thrust it toward Hades, and an enormous wave rose up from the sea and crashed against the stone barrier that Hades had created.

"I cannot let you do this!" Poseidon shouted. "It is against the order of things."

"I was created for this. It *is* the order." Hades' voice carried on a roar across the waves.

Poseidon tried sending another wave at Hades, this one far larger. It curled overhead, the water forming a terrifying wall that loomed above us. Fear iced the blood in my veins.

Hades' magic surged stronger, and his wall of rocks curved up, arcing over us. As the wave crashed against his wall of boulders, he looked back at me and roared, "Run!"

I did as he commanded, sprinting across the narrow strip of land that led toward the portal. In addition to the tidal waves he was creating, Poseidon had stirred up the sea. The gray waves crashed ferociously against the stone walls that plunged into the water on either side of me. They splashed up, soaking me, but I didn't slow. Out of the corner of my eye, I could see Poseidon watching me.

He raised a hand, and his magic flared, smelling of the salty sea and feeling like a rush of cold water against my skin. A wave rose up in front of him, coming right at me.

"No!" Hades yelled, and rocks rose up between me and the wave that bore down upon me, creating an impenetrable wall. Poseidon's attack slammed right into it, but it held strong.

I glanced back at Hades, realizing that he had directed all of his energy toward me, and the rock wall in front of him had disappeared. His gaze was on me, dark with worry.

Poseidon noticed the hole in his defense and directed another wave toward him.

No!

"Hades!" I screamed. "Look out!"

But it was too late. The wave crashed over him, dragging him into the sea. Fear lanced me, rage on its heels. How dare Poseidon?

My magic swelled within me, searching for any forms of plant life. I could feel it in the hills around me, the scrubby grasses and stunted bushes.

They would do no good.

I reached into the sea, searching for the weeds that would surely grow beneath the depths. I found them, feeling my magic surge through my veins as I called for them. Though they were part of Poseidon's watery domain, they obeyed me and rose.

I directed them toward the terrifying sea god, and the dark green weeds grew quickly, shooting from the depths. I felt the plants wrap around his limbs as if they were part of my own body. As they dragged him down in the water, the darkness inside me surged to life.

His roar was the last thing I heard, and the darkness inside me *delighted* in what I'd just done, flaring with joy and power. It surged through me, so heady that I almost swooned.

Suddenly, I felt invincible. Beneath the surface of the sea, I could feel Poseidon struggling against my grasp.

I smiled darkly and tightened the vines. I couldn't drown him, of course. But I could tear him apart.

Tear him apart.

The words echoed in my mind, and deep in my soul, I felt the faintest objection. It rose, fighting to the surface until it screamed within me.

I couldn't tear him apart. I couldn't tear *anyone* apart. That was awful.

I struggled against the urge, feeling the lust for power scream inside me.

It's not me.

I repeated the mantra, trying to separate my conscious mind from the desire that roared inside me. I didn't have to obey it. I didn't have to be that person.

It took everything I had to shove down the urge to rend Poseidon limb from limb. I held him tight below the surface but didn't harm him. But I wouldn't be able to hold him for long. If I wanted any shot at defeating a god, I'd have to fight with everything I had.

Unfortunately for me, everything I had meant letting the darkness take control and do unforgivable things.

Instead, I focused on Hades. I spun back to look for him, searching the crashing sea.

A half second later, he shot up from the depths, his golden wings carrying him high into the air. His gaze landed on me, and he swooped down, gripping me around the waist and hauling me up.

I clung to his neck as he flew low to the ground, heading toward the portal that would take us back to his realm. His face was set in lines of determination, and the wind blew fiercely as we hurtled through the air.

We reached the portal just as Poseidon broke free of my weeds. He rode toward us on a massive wave, but Hades plowed through the portal to his realm, bringing me with him.

I clung to him as the ether spun us through space and spat us out. The familiar scent of the underworld enveloped me, brimstone and fire strangely welcoming despite the dreary light that shrouded everything in gray.

Hades landed at a run, not letting me go as he sprinted toward the gates to his realm.

"You can put me down!" I shouted.

"Not safe yet." He launched himself into the air to fly toward the gate.

From the other side of the gate, Cerberus watched us, concern in his eyes. He stiffened and growled low in his throat.

I looked back, spotting Poseidon hurtling through the portal and into the Underworld. He looked out of place with his gleaming silver-blue armor and the water that surged around his feet.

"He can come here?" Shock lanced me.

Hades didn't respond, just flew faster toward the gate.

We were nearly there when Poseidon shot several sharp jets of water toward us. They flew like spears, and two of them pierced Hades in the back.

He grunted, nearly dropping me, but tightened his grip as he flew through the gates. I searched his face, horrified to see it twisted in lines of pain, his skin pale.

I looked back and spotted Poseidon standing on the far side of the gates, staring into Hades' realm. Cerberus lunged at him, all three heads barking, and Poseidon disappeared back through the portal.

Hades stumbled to his knees as he landed, and as his arms loosened, I tumbled to the ground. His wings disappeared as I cupped his face and raised his head to force him to meet my gaze.

"Are you all right?" I looked around to see his armor torn open as if a spear had punctured him. Through the holes in his metal, I could see jagged flesh and red blood. Horror chilled me. "Hades! Your back."

"It will heal." His voice was rough with pain. "Just needs time."

Cerberus lumbered toward us, then sat on his haunches near Hades and watched him with concern.

"How long will it take?" I asked. "Can I do anything?"

"I'm fine." He grimaced and struggled to stand, rising until he towered over me.

I climbed to my feet. "What was that all about?"

"The other gods do not want me to succeed, so they take every opportunity they can to stop me."

Understanding dawned. "Poseidon was stronger out there because we were by the sea."

"Precisely. And he was able to walk in the neutral zone near the River Styx."

I turned back to the gate, inspecting it warily. "But he couldn't enter your realm. Not like Zeus could."

"If he really wanted to, he could. But he'd be weakened. And he doesn't like Cerberus."

"Doesn't like Cerberus?" I dropped my jaw in mock shock. "The monster."

A rare smile tugged at the corner of Hades' mouth. "A monster."

"Where can we go to rest? You look like you need it."

"I'm fine."

"You're really not. And I could use a break as well."

He nodded stiffly. "There is a guard tower near here. It is generally unused, so it should be empty."

I held up my hand to gesture forward. "Lead the way."

He nodded and turned, striding through the forest back toward the gate. Cerberus gave a low woof and jumped up, following alongside. I stole glances at the enormous dog. He was both adorable and terrifying. When I caught sight of Echo riding on one of his heads, I adjusted my assessment more toward adorable.

"Here." Hades stopped in front of a stone tower that

was built right into the massive wall surrounding his realm. It rose three stories tall, with the entrance on the second story. A set of narrow wooden stairs led to the door. He climbed them, and I followed. At the top, he pushed open the wooden door to reveal a simple round room with a hearth on one side and a table in the middle. Dust gathered in the corners, and spiderwebs crowded the ceiling.

I stepped inside, warily checking the corners for an army of rats. "Very...rustic."

He huffed a low laugh, seeming almost surprised by it. "I'm not sure what you were expecting from the underworld."

"Well, you're the king of hell. Perhaps a bit more luxury."

He looked at me, seeming genuinely confused. "What would I do with that?"

"Never mind." Hades was definitely the sort who would prefer to rough it, no question. His entire life was about duty, and that certainly didn't involve fancy accommodation. Hell, this was a step up from the cave where we'd spent time before.

He waved a hand toward the hearth, and a fire burst to life, crackling with a warm and cheery light. Despite the festive nature of the fire, the extra illumination highlighted the many spiders staring at me with multifaceted eyes. They were slightly creepy, and I shivered.

"Do you want me to banish them?" he asked.

I frowned. I *did* want that, just a little. But I could also feel the life in them, my magic reaching out to touch them in a way that was becoming more and more familiar.

They meant me no harm. If I'd been a tiny fly, they wouldn't have hesitated to wrap me up in their webs and eat me. But as it was, they were merely curious.

"No, it's fine," I said. "This is their home."

He nodded, then strode to the fire, his movements stiff.

"Here," I said, "let me help."

I hurried to him and reached for the armor at his back. He stiffened and turned to me. "What are you doing?"

"Helping?"

"Why?"

"You were hurt protecting me."

"I was hurt escaping."

"You could have just flown out of there more quickly and left me to take the hit."

"I need you for my plans."

I frowned at him. "That's true. But I think you're just being a jerk to try to drive me off."

He shrugged, his gaze impassive.

"Well, turn around and face the fire while I get this off of you."

He heaved a sigh and did as I commanded, facing

the warm blaze. It took me a moment to figure out the clasps on the armor, but finally, I had them undone. I pulled off the massively heavy metal plates and set them aside, then saw that his shirt was heavily coated in blood.

"Is there anywhere you can take a bath here?" I asked. "You're absolutely soaked."

He nodded, pulling the shirt over his head to reveal his wounds. Two gaping holes cut into his flesh, put there by the sheer force of the water. As I watched, they healed, closing up as if they'd never been there at all. They didn't leave so much as a bruise behind.

And yet, he still had the scars that I'd seen on him in the bathing chamber. The dark tattoos that decorated his skin couldn't hide the long marks that had once been terrible gashes.

I raised a hand, helpless to stop myself, and ran my fingertips over the once torn flesh. He flinched as I did so but didn't pull away.

"What made these, if Poseidon's magic can't leave a mark on you?"

His shoulders bowed slightly, then straightened. "Nothing."

He stepped away from me.

"It can't be nothing." I moved forward, following him.

"It's nothing." He walked toward an arched doorway at the back of the room, heading down a set of stone steps that wrapped around the edge of the tower.

I trailed him, entering a room at the base of the tower that looked a lot like his bathroom back at his castle. The space was made up almost entirely of a deep bathing pool set right into the ground. Steam spiraled from it, and I watched him strip off the rest of his clothes. The sight of him took my breath away as he climbed into the water. It rose up around his calves and thighs, covering his muscular buttocks and waist. When he was deep enough, he dipped himself entirely in the water, rising up from the depths with his skin washed clean of blood.

I wanted nothing more than to climb in with him.

And why shouldn't I?

Sure, I was angry with him. Mad as hell, in fact. He drove me insane, and he'd committed plenty of wrongs against me.

He'd also taken me to learn about my past. As a result, I had seen Nana again. According to her, I had the power to save him. I would save both of us by going to the site of doomsday. It sounded crazy, but after what I'd experienced at the pit of darkness beneath his castle, I had so much reason to believe he was better than all of that. He'd never had a chance to learn right from wrong. He'd literally been crafted from *wrong*. And yet, there was still good inside him, fighting its way to the surface as he tried to do the right thing. There were some definite missteps on his part, but he was trying.

If one of my girlfriends had told me that she was attempting to change her arsehole boyfriend, I'd have told her she was insane. And it probably *was* insane what I was trying. Men didn't change.

But Hades wasn't a man. He was a god.

And I was going to try. Not just to save him and the world, but because I wanted to. Because I truly believed there was more to Hades. When we were together like this, I could feel the light rise in him.

I pulled my jacket off, then my shirt, tossing them to the side. My bra went next, followed by my boots and trousers. By the time I was stark naked, Hades had turned around.

16

Hades

Seraphia stood at the edge of the pool, every piece of her clothing lying in a pile at her feet. My mouth went dry at the sight of her, at the miraculous vision she created.

She couldn't be real.

No one could look like that.

Long legs and full hips, a tiny waist and small breasts tipped with pink. Her dark hair fell in waves down her back, gleaming in the light of the torches that had flickered to life when I'd entered the room.

I felt my body go unbearably hard as she stepped toward the water. Desperate desire raced through me, so fierce it stole my breath. My hands itched to touch her, to grip her hips and run over the curve of her waist.

She put one foot on the first step, and my throat tightened.

I should get out. I should let her have the pool to herself.

But that wasn't what she wanted. From the way her green eyes traveled over my form, bright with hunger, she didn't want to be alone in this pool.

I groaned low. "If you get into this pool, Seraphia, I will not keep my hands off of you."

She smiled and kept walking. The water rose up around her knees and thighs, and I was grateful for the magic that kept it perpetually clean. Nothing but the finest things should touch her skin.

I'd warned her once. I wouldn't warn her again.

The water closed up over her hips, and I strode toward her, cutting through the water.

"You fought for me," I said, something in my chest clutching at the memory. "Used your magic to drag Poseidon into his cursed sea."

She nodded, her gaze on mine. Heat burned within her eyes so brightly that it burned me in turn. When she stopped in front of me, I reached for her, grabbing her waist and pulling her forward.

Her body pressed full length to mine, so warm and smooth that my head spun from the pleasure of it. I'd never touched another like this, skin to skin, body to body. It was so intense that for the briefest moment, my mind went entirely blank.

Then she tilted her head up, her lips slightly parted. An aching groan tore from my throat, and I bent to kiss her, taking her lips with a roughness that would have bothered me if she hadn't wrapped her arms around my neck and kissed me back, moaning against my mouth.

She tasted of sweetness and light, and I couldn't get enough of her, my tongue delving deep. I ran my hands down the long sweep of her sides, my palms tingling as I touched her.

"Hades," she murmured. "I want you."

The words lit me on fire. With her scent wrapping around me and her touch burning into me, it was impossible to resist her.

I wanted to know every inch of her. Taste every inch.

Possessiveness ran through me, so fierce it almost made my head spin.

Mine.

"Seraphia." I said her name like a prayer as I picked her up and carried her to the few steps to the edge of the pool. I sat her on the edge and stepped between her thighs. They bracketed my hips, the smooth skin burning into me.

She gasped, her hands digging into my shoulders as her gaze met mine.

All of my control was stripped away. It had always been something upon which I prided myself, but she tore it to pieces and burned it to ashes.

I cupped her breasts, the skin so smooth and perfect that I wanted more. I wanted to feel her beneath my lips.

Unable to stop myself, I dipped my mouth to her chest, running my tongue over the smooth skin of her breasts. Over the tight peaks that strained toward me.

"Hades." She sounded nearly breathless, and it sent a thrill through me.

Yes.

Pleasing her like this sent a deep, unfamiliar wave of satisfaction through me. When her hands came up to grip my hair, I groaned low in my throat, helpless in her thrall.

"I want more of you," I growled against the inner curve of her breast.

"Yes," she gasped.

I gripped her hips as I ran my tongue down her stomach, drawn to the sweet core of her that had haunted my dreams since I'd last touched her. I craved her with every ounce of my being, wanting nothing more than to drown in her taste, her scent.

My knees hit the floor of the pool without a second thought, my shoulders pushing her thighs apart. The sight of her made my head spin, made me forget everything but her.

I was all instinct. All desire. My voice was gravel as it left my throat. "I'm going to taste you now."

She gasped, stilling, and I gripped her hips as I lowered my mouth to the softness that beckoned me.

Her hands tightened in my hair as I swept my tongue over her, devouring her like I couldn't get enough.

I *couldn't*.

I'd never be able to.

I wanted this every day for the rest of my days, and the idea that I might not have it made desperate dread curl through me. I'd make her feel so good, she'd never leave me.

The taste of her made my head spin and pleasure coil tight.

As I kissed her, she gasped, and her back arched. I worshiped at the altar of her reactions, following each one to learn what made her tremble and what made her move against my mouth.

Her hands tightened in my hair, and the sweet sting sent a spike of pleasure straight to my cock. I could feel the tension within her, and my body reacted, feeling bound to her by something I couldn't control. I was ravenous, a starving beast that couldn't get enough of the sweetness before me.

Her thighs clenched, and she cried out, trembling fiercely as the pleasure overtook her. The feeling of her moving beneath me and clutching my hair dragged me over the edge as well. I was unable to control the waves of terrible pleasure that racked my body.

I'd never felt anything like it, so all-encompassing that I became one with Seraphia. One with the light. It was the most miraculous thing I'd ever felt, enough to spin my consciousness out into the heavens.

When it was over, I rested my head against her inner thigh, panting.

I'd spilled into the pool like a boy. Like a *human.*

The idea was abhorrent.

"Hades?" Her hand tightened in my hair, and I straightened, looking down on her.

She sat up, her cheeks flushed and her hair wild. "That was...amazing."

I wanted more of it already. More of her.

The desire gripped me hard, not just my body, but my soul.

I wanted her more than I wanted the darkness. She made the light rise within me, and even though it was painful, I wanted it.

No.

Shocked with my own thoughts, I stepped backward, surging through the water.

How had she done this to me, so quickly converted my thoughts to her own desires? Was I that much a fool?

I spun from her and charged out of the water, calling upon my magic as I went. Clothing draped my form, the usual leather armor that I wore when at home. It formed a greatly needed barrier between her gaze and my skin.

Without looking back, I strode up the stairs toward the main part of the tower, needing space from her.

Needing to recommit myself to my cause. If only we were back at my castle, where I could revisit the darkness to be reminded of my purpose.

As if on cue, my hands tingled. I stripped off a glove to look at my right hand and found it partially transparent.

I was running out of time.

Seraphia

Hurt sliced through me as I watched Hades disappear into the stairwell. Heart pounding, I turned back to the pool and stared at the dark water.

How had that just happened? Both the sex and the aftermath?

I shook my head. What had I been thinking?

I'd known how torn he was. Of course he wouldn't turn to my side after one amazing sexual encounter. It wasn't like I was going to cure him with my magic vagina, after all.

But with every moment together, I felt him coming over to my side little by little. I wasn't imagining things.

Quickly, I dressed. My stomach grumbled, and I was forced to ascend the stairs in search of sustenance. And Hades.

Mostly Hades.

I found him in the main room, unpacking the leather satchel that had been on Horse's back. He handed me a small parcel wrapped in paper, and I took it.

Since I had no idea of how to talk about what had just happened, I decided that ignoring it was the best bet. He certainly was. Despite the flush on his cheeks, everything about him appeared normal, as if it had never happened.

I could start a fight and demand to know how he could do those things with me—make me feel like that —then completely turn it off and return to ice. But that would be pointless and needlessly painful, so I tried to ignore the hurt as I unwrapped the food and asked, "What next?"

"After you eat, we will sleep to regain our energy. And then we will seek the answers that I require."

"About the time and location of doomsday?"

He nodded sharply, and I sat at the small wooden table, my mind spinning.

Of course, that was the next step of his plan, and so he would pursue it. But in the last few hours, I'd managed to make myself forget. Just a little bit.

My gaze flicked up to his as I debated my options.

"You're coming with me, Seraphia. You agreed." His tone brooked no argument, and I didn't bother making any.

"You're right."

He frowned. "You're making this too easy."

I shrugged, assembling a sandwich from the cheese and bread inside the parcel he'd given me. "No, I'm not. I'm just doing what I said I would do."

"You're going to try to stop me, though."

I took a bite of the sandwich and mulled it over. "I'm not sure that I have to *stop* you, do I? I just have to resist doing what you want me to do."

"But can you?" he asked.

I nodded, thinking back to Poseidon. I'd resisted the urge to tear him apart. It'd been so strong that it had nearly taken me to my knees, but I'd resisted.

The slightest worry tugged at the edge of my consciousness, though. I'd been tested several times now, and though I'd always succeeded in the end, it hadn't grown any easier. If the motivation were right, could I possibly succumb?

No.

There couldn't be a motivation that would make me use my power to suck all the life from the earth. That was a twisted version of the Persephone tale, and I wouldn't fall prey to it.

"I'll be fine." I looked at him, watching the way the glow of the fire flickered across his fallen angel's features.

How could he look so impossibly beautiful when he was capable of such terrible things? When he'd been created by such evil? Was that the joke—that the destroyer of the world would look like the angel who had come to save it?

"Did you know that the Oracle of Kamarina was my grandmother?" I asked.

He frowned. "She was?"

That answered that. I nodded.

"Is that good?" he asked.

"Very." Despite the pain he'd caused me, my heart hurt for the idea that he wouldn't realize that seeing a family member was a good thing. He'd never had anyone like that to want to see again. I finished my sandwich under his watchful gaze, exhaustion tugging at me. Weary, I stood. "I'm going to sleep."

He nodded, and I turned away. I had no idea where I was going, but there had to be one other level to this place, and I was going to go there and hope there'd be a bed.

When I reached the top floor and saw the moderately sized bed, my shoulders sagged with exhausted gratitude. Quickly, I shucked off my clothes, leaving only my underwear and shirt, then crawled beneath the covers. The sheets felt clean enough, and I was too tired to really care.

Sleep came quickly, followed by dreams of Hades that made me burn with a fire that wanted to consume me.

17

SERAPHIA

I woke wrapped in Hades' arms. I stiffened briefly, then relaxed back against him, lulled by the warmth and strength of his touch.

It felt so damned good.

Except...

Last night, we'd parted on pretty freaking terrible terms.

He had joined me in the bed a while after I'd fallen asleep. I'd woken just long enough to notice him staying on his own side, perfectly still. Sometime in the night, he must have reached out for me. Unconsciously, for sure.

Was he still asleep behind me, though? Or was he awake?

I peeked back.

As if he felt his gaze on me, his eyelashes fluttered open. Confusion flickered in the depths of his sea-blue eyes, then he sat up. His face turned impassive, and he rose from the bed. The tattoos on his bare chest drew my eye, and though I wanted to ask about them, I resisted.

"It is time to leave." There wasn't a flicker of emotion in his voice, but his gaze slid briefly to me and then away, as if he were unable to help himself.

I nodded and stood, turning away from him as I pulled on my clothes. Considering that I was half naked, this could have been a good opportunity to get under his skin again. But I didn't have it in me. After his quick rejection last night, there was no way I was putting myself in that situation again, no matter how temporarily amazing it had been.

Though I didn't hear him dress, I was suddenly alone.

Echo fluttered in front of me, and I smiled. "Where were you last night? With your new friend?" The little bat flew in a circle, and I took it to be a yes. "Well, I'm glad one of us had a good night. Come on."

I went toward the stairs. When I reached the door, a squawking noise caught my attention. My heart leapt, and I spun around. "Beatrix?"

The black raven sat on the windowsill, feathers gleaming despite the dull light outside. She flew into the room and transformed into Beatrix, who grinned widely. "Took me ages to find you."

I ran to her and gave her a quick hug. "Thank you for coming."

"I have news." Her tone sobered.

My stomach pitched. "Yes?"

She reached into the tiny pocket of her brilliant blue leggings and pulled out a little vial. "This is the potion that will break the pomegranate curse and allow you to leave. *But*...it must be blessed by Hades."

"What?" My skin chilled.

"He has to agree to your freedom."

"Shit." I crossed my arms over my chest, my limbs suddenly tingling with anxiety.

"Exactly." She gripped my arm. "I'm sorry. This isn't much better than your situation before."

I drew in an unsteady breath. "It is, though. He said he didn't know a way to break the pomegranate potion, so before this, I had nothing. Now I've got something. Maybe. But how is he supposed to bless it?"

"He must hold the potion and give his consent to you leaving."

Damn. It would be hard to trick him into doing that. I sucked in a steadying breath and nodded my head. "Okay. I can work with that. It's better than what I had before."

"Which was nothing." Beatrix shrugged. "So yeah, it's better."

I took the vial from her and stuck it in my pocket. "I'm going to have to make him a seriously compelling deal to get him to do this for me."

"Any ideas?"

"Besides bringing about the apocalypse? No. Because that's top of his wish list."

"You sure landed a weird one."

I pursed my lips and nodded. "I wouldn't stand a chance without you guys working to help me on the outside, so thank you."

"Of course." She hugged me tightly. "I'm going to go, but I also wanted to tell you that Eve is still looking for another way to get you the hell out of here. Mac and Carrow, too."

"Thank you." I prayed she'd be successful, because I just couldn't imagine trying to get Hades to consent to me leaving. Not unless I'd already destroyed the earth first.

She nodded, then stepped backward, transformed into a raven, and swept out into the muted daylight.

I drew in a bracing breath and turned for the door, already debating how I was going to ask Hades. I'd need to wait for the right opportunity, that was certain. But what would it be? And was there any way to delay what I was supposed to do with him today?

I reached the main level and found Hades standing

in front of the hearth, staring into the flames. An idea popped into my head. "I don't have complete control of my magic yet. So we need to keep training before I can go with you to find what you're looking for."

He turned to me, one eyebrow raised skeptically. "Really? You dragged Poseidon himself under the waves of his own sea, and you think you don't have control?"

Hmm. When he put it that way...I was doing all right.

I frowned at him and crossed my arms over my chest. "Fine. But I'm not going to help you when it really counts. You can never make me suck all the life from the earth."

"We'll see." His tone was cryptic as he turned toward the door.

I followed him outside, finding Cerberus sleeping by the base of the tower. He was so big that I could touch his head from here, even though it was resting on the ground.

"Where to next?" I asked.

"We will be going to the Place of Memories."

I waited a beat for him to continue. When he didn't, I said, "Aaand?"

At the base of the stairs, he turned back to me. "And what?"

"What's there?"

"I've never been." He turned back to the forest.

"Now you're being purposefully obtuse. Tell me what you know. Do you think I won't want to go?"

His shoulders moved with a sigh, and he turned back. "Of course I think you won't want to go. But if you insist on knowing, I'll tell you. The Place of Memories is dangerous, but it's also valuable. It is a temple where we might be able to speak to the most ancient of my race—the Titans."

"Weren't they locked away in Tartarus?"

He nodded, his gaze shifting slightly, as if he didn't want to talk about this. Was *that* why he'd tried to avoid the conversation? He didn't like discussing Tartarus? But why? Before I could ask, he continued. "Their memories are stored away there, as shadows of their former selves. If we ask the correct questions, we can get the answers we need."

"Why didn't we go there before?"

"Because you were not strong enough."

"So you really think I'm strong enough to face a *Titan*?"

Something flashed on his face, and he stepped toward me, gripping my bicep firmly. "Yes, Seraphia. I would not put you at risk."

I swallowed hard at the protective fierceness in his eyes. "Don't you realize you put my soul at risk by trying to force me to do that? It will tear me apart if I fall to the darkness and do what you want me to do."

His dark gaze searched mine, no doubt looking for

the truth of my words. There was *so* much truth there. How could he not see that?

"It won't feel as bad as you think it will," he said.

"You feel terrible all the time, don't you?"

"That's because of the light inside me."

"No, it's the conflict. And you're choosing the wrong side."

He pulled back and spun away. "We will not discuss this now. Come."

Pissed, I hurried after him, matching him stride for stride as we walked toward the gate. "Will we be bothered by your brothers where we're going?"

"They are not my brothers."

"Really? The myths were wrong?"

He said nothing, just kept walking toward the gate, and I had to wonder if they actually *were* his bothers, and he just didn't want to claim them as his own. Considering how they attacked him on sight, I couldn't blame him.

I kept pace with him. "So do we need to be on the alert for attack? Because godly attacks are well outside the realm of my usual abilities. A little warning would be nice."

"Anything is possible, though they wouldn't expect me to be leaving my realm again so soon."

I nodded, hoping to avoid them. I didn't want to give my magic any more chances to turn dark.

You must go with him...

Nana's words echoed in my head. I'd have listened to her, no matter what, but now that I knew she was an ancient oracle...

Of course I had to go. To prove myself.

I shivered, not liking the sound of that.

Did I believe her?

Yes.

She'd never lie to me. Still, what if she'd interpreted it wrong?

It wouldn't matter. Either way, I had to at least go with Hades to our next destination.

Hades stopped at the gates and stared out. Cerberus joined him, the massive dog standing at his side and watching through the gate as well. In a seemingly unconscious gesture, Hades placed a hand on the dog's side, and Cerberus heaved a great sigh and leaned into him.

My heart twisted in my chest.

Hades was changing. There was no question that he was slowly beginning to turn to the light, even if I was only able to witness it in small moments like these.

I joined them, inspecting the shadowy landscape in front of us. Hardly any light came from the gray sky, and the River Styx moved sluggishly through the fields of wheat. I searched for any sign of Poseidon in the forest or on the mountain to the right, though I saw nothing.

"Are we going through the same gate?" I asked.

He shook his head. "We must go to Charon."

"The boatman?" I shivered. "We're riding in the boat of the dead?"

"Yes."

Oh, shit.

Hades

I could feel Seraphia's gaze burning into me as I stepped forward and called upon Horse and Styx. The two mounts appeared in front of us, and Seraphia lunged backward, clearly surprised.

"You can just *do* that?" she asked. "Call them to you?"

"In my realm, yes." I gestured to Styx. "Would you like help up?"

She frowned, clearly wanting to say no, but there weren't any convenient stairs to give her a boost. Finally, she nodded.

As soon as my hands went around her waist, I was sent back to the previous night in the pool. Heat flushed through me, and I forced myself to think of the cold sea outside my castle.

Finally, she was seated, and I could release her. My palms felt empty and cold as I let go.

"Thanks." Her voice was tight, and I wondered if she was thinking of the same things I was.

How could she not? That had been the most incredible thing I'd ever done.

No.

I couldn't think of it. It distracted me from my goals. Worse, it turned me toward the light. Fractured me, as the darkness had said.

I spun from her and mounted Horse, then nudged the animal forward. He picked up the pace, and soon, we were racing across the field to the River Styx.

As I rode, every inch of me was attuned to the presence of Seraphia at my side. Somehow, she was squeezing herself inside my soul, setting up residence in my thoughts, no matter how hard I tried to ignore her.

After roughly twenty minutes, we neared the river. Charon saw us and directed his small boat toward the shoreline. When Seraphia and I reached the bank, I leapt off Horse and went back to her, helping her dismount. I touched her as little as possible, but still, my blood leapt.

I waved my hand, and the horses disappeared. Together, we walked toward the riverbank. The clear, dark water moved slowly, smelling bright and fresh, and the grass was springy beneath my feet. I rarely noticed such things, but with Seraphia nearby, I was unable to ignore them.

It was strange, how she made me feel more alive.

At the riverbank, Seraphia leaned slightly toward me

as Charon approached. She stared at the boatman, her face pale, and I tried to see him through her eyes.

From the perspective of a mortal, he must appear quite ominous. He stood at the bow of the wooden boat, the long punt gripped in his hands as he drove it into the water and pushed off the bottom to move forward. He was a skeletal figure, despite the black robes that cloaked him from crown to feet. It was impossible to see through the robes, but when he moved, it was obvious that he was made of nothing but bones.

He stopped the boat at the riverbank and bowed to me, his ragged dark cloak swaying in the breeze.

"Charon." I inclined my head slightly.

As was customary, he said nothing. Instead, he held out his hand.

I reached into a pocket and withdrew two coins, then handed them over. I could feel Seraphia's eyes on me as I did so, and looked at her to say, "He requires payment."

"Even from the king of hell?"

"Even I am not immune to death." I felt a slightly bitter smile tug at my mouth. "Though it would be very difficult for me to achieve such a state."

She frowned at me. "Why would you want to?"

After so long in this existence? Why wouldn't I?

Her.

The answer was so clear and obvious. It wasn't that I had a death wish—far from it. But I did have a wish for things to be different. To break the endless cycle of darkness, disappearance, torture, and rebirth.

But that's what we were here to do, wasn't it?

The idea calmed something inside me. We were on our way to accomplishing my goals, at long last.

I gestured toward the boat and held out a hand. "You may enter."

She ignored my hand and stepped aboard herself, watching Charon warily. He'd already turned his attention toward the river, though.

I followed her onto the boat and said to Charon, "We may go."

Instead of cutting across the river, Charon moved forward, heading down the wide, winding path of still, dark water.

"Where will this take us?" Seraphia asked. "Does it go directly to the Place of Memories?"

I nodded. "The Place of Memories is located in the middle of all the gods' territories. It is truly a neutral zone. We are each able to access it by different methods, however, and mine is via the River Styx. Though I've never had cause to use it myself."

"And Poseidon comes from the sea?"

I nodded. "The sea touches the Place of Memories, and he can walk up from the depths. Zeus will descend from the sky, and Athena can ride her horse across the plains."

"What about me? Shouldn't I have my own access?"

I looked at her, considering. "That is a very good point." She was so much stronger than she had been, and one day, she would fully ascend as a goddess.

It would be magnificent.

Still, I didn't know where her access would be. "For now, you will approach with me."

She nodded and turned to the water, staring down into the darkness. A few moments later, she jumped, startled. "There are people in there."

"Souls." I leaned over to look, spotting one of the wispy white figures. "They have yet to decide whether they truly want to enter the afterlife."

"So they just swim around down there?"

"I would not call it swimming, precisely. They exist in a state of indecision."

She grimaced. "Sounds terrible."

I shrugged. It was the way of things. Everything was terrible here, but a person got used to it.

As Charon punted us forward, the riverbank passed on either side, moving slowly by as the grass waved in the faint wind. We left behind Cerberus and the gate, the mountain that housed Lachesis, and the forests.

An hour later, Seraphia pointed toward the building that rose ahead of us, sitting high on a hill. "Is that it?"

I nodded. The temple was a massive rectangle, built of the traditional columns favored by the ancient Greeks. The gods built in the same way the humans had long ago, and this was a construction of their own making.

The sky was dark gray overhead, with the faintest glow of orange from where the sun fought to break through. Charon took us as far as he could, dropping us at the riverbank roughly a ten-minute walk from the temple.

"Thank you." I disembarked, then turned back to offer Seraphia my hand.

After a brief hesitation, she took it, and I couldn't help the sense of satisfaction that shot through me. Gracefully, she stepped off the boat and stared at the temple in front of us. The columns were as white as bone, symmetrical and stark against the gray sky.

A great chasm separated us from the hill, crossed by a narrow swinging bridge. She eyed it with trepidation. "We have to cross *that?*"

I nodded. "All must prove worthy to cross."

"What the heck does that mean?"

"It is different for everyone, but you will see." I turned to her. "I have faith you will be up to the challenge."

Understanding dawned in her eyes. "It's going to test my magic, isn't it?"

"And your strength."

"That's why you trained me."

"And because I want you to be able to protect yourself. To become the goddess I know you are."

She frowned, crossing her arms over her chest as she stared at the bridge. "Yeah, yeah." She shook herself, seeming to drive away whatever nerves she felt, then started forward. A half second later, she hesitated and turned back. "Actually, if I am going to face this risk, I want something in return."

"What?"

She reached into her pocket and held out a small vial of potion. "This potion will break the curse of the pomegranate that you put on me. I will be able to leave your realm without feeling excruciating pain, *if* you bless it and give your approval."

Shock lanced me. "That is possible?"

"Apparently."

I cursed inwardly. I'd always assumed there was no cure, but that was my arrogance getting the better of me. "You have already agreed to do this with me. I will not make another concession. Certainly not one so great."

She scowled. "I won't go."

"It's too late now." I gripped her arm firmly, but not hard enough to bruise. "Now come."

She shoved the potion back in her pocket. "I'm going to get you to agree."

"Not now, you're not."

She gave me a hard look, and for the briefest moment, it was possible to believe that she could accomplish it.

Together, we strode toward the bridge. It was narrow

and ancient, the wooden slats held together by frayed rope. Below, the crevasse plunged into endless darkness.

"I'm not crossing that," Seraphia said.

"Yes, you are." I turned to her, trying to imbue my voice with the confidence I felt in her. "I would not risk your life. Not in a thousand years. You will be fine."

She frowned, her gaze darting to the crevasse. "That looks like the stuff of nightmares."

"It is. You must prove yourself worthy to visit the Place of Memories."

"Yeah, yeah. You go first."

I nodded. "Remember, if you see me face a challenge while crossing, yours will likely not be the same."

"It's personalized. I get it."

"Precisely." I still gripped her forearms, and I couldn't help but run my thumbs over her biceps. "You're strong enough for this, Seraphia. I promise it."

She nodded, her gaze glued to mine. For the briefest moment, I felt what the Oracle of Kamarina had said—we were two halves of a whole. When I looked into her eyes, I sensed the connection like a chain that bound us together.

I would do anything not to sever it.

The thought shocked me, but it felt so true that it could have been written in the stars, the same way my destiny had been.

And yet, it was my destiny that could tear us apart.

18

Seraphia

I stared up at Hades, caught by the look in his eyes. The intensity there took my breath away, and I had no idea how to process it.

From behind me, thunder struck, the boom making my bones shake.

I turned, my heart in my throat. "Zeus?"

The memory of the fearsome god hit me hard. Hades had defeated him the last time we'd encountered him, but it had been difficult. Their armies had clashed, and I'd nearly died in the crossfire.

I'd protected myself.

I needed to remember that. And I was stronger now. There was no need to be afraid.

Well, maybe there was. But I had a good chance of coming out alive, at least.

"Perhaps." Hades stepped away from me and stared out over the crevasse toward the temple. "It could be just a storm."

"We should get this over with." I shivered, feeling the danger on the air.

He nodded. "I will go first. When I have crossed, you may follow."

"Alone?"

He turned back to me and nodded. "You will prove yourself. Do not worry. But whatever you do—you *must* get across. Do not deviate."

I swallowed hard. There was nowhere to deviate to. I either crossed the bridge or I fell off.

I was *so* not keen on falling off.

Hades stepped toward the bridge, his dark cloak whipping in the wind behind him. He hesitated briefly, then whirled back to face me, gripping my arms tight. He looked like he wanted to bite his words back but couldn't stop himself from speaking, and his gaze burned into mine. "I won't let *anything* happen to you. I promise."

I swallowed hard and nodded, unable to look away from him. I didn't want anyone fighting my battles for me. But his protectiveness kindled a flame inside me, warm and fierce. There was just something about him now. Maybe it had been last night, maybe not, but he was different. His whole focus was on me, as if I were the most precious thing in the world.

He'd never let anything happen to me.

I would protect him, too.

I knew it like I knew my own face in the mirror. He was something to me. I didn't want him to be, and I certainly didn't like some of the things he'd done to me, but after seeing into the darkness and feeling how his soul fought it...well, he was worth protecting, too.

The words wouldn't leave my lips, though. I couldn't say them back to him, and I wasn't even sure whether he wanted to hear them.

He gave me one last look, then strode toward the cliff. The narrow bridge rattled when he stepped on it, but he didn't slow his stride or bother to grip the rope handrails for support.

The wind was fiercer through the crevasse, and his cloak whipped wildly to the right, his dark hair blowing with it. As he neared the middle of the bridge, the clouds overhead darkened. They rolled through the sky, gathering overhead. Magic sparked within them, so fierce that it prickled my skin.

I hurried to the edge of the cliff, watching as the lighting struck through the dark clouds. One of the brilliant bolts flashed close to Hades, and my heart thundered.

They would hit him!

Hades raised one of his glove-sheathed hands, and

his bident appeared. It gleamed under the crack of lightning, and I could smell his firelight magic from here.

When the second bolt of lightning shot from the sky, it headed right for him. He pointed the bident directly at it, and a shadow burst from the prongs. Huge and black, it looked like a shadowy grim reaper as it flew through the air toward the lightning bolt. The two collided, and Hades' reaper gleamed with bright light for the briefest moment. It seemed to suck in the energy from the lightning bolt and double in size before it flew toward the clouds and disappeared into them.

Lightning flickered erratically within the clouds, as if they were trying to fight off the shadow of death that had surged into their midst.

Below, Hades kept walking, his powerful strides eating up the length of the bridge as he hurried toward the other side. Movement from the cliff opposite me caught my eye, and I spotted eight enormous warriors charging toward the swaying bridge. They sprinted onto the wooden slats and ran toward Hades, their huge swords raised high as ancient armor clanked around their bodies.

Through the massive metal helmets, I could see that their eyes glowed with an unholy green fire. They were far larger than normal men—bigger even than Hades himself. The mere sight of them made me shiver to the base of my soul.

Was *this* what I would have to fight?

It didn't bother Hades. He just drew a sword from the ether and raised his bident high, then charged toward the monsters as they ran at him. My heart stuck in my throat as I watched him cut them down one by one, never hesitating.

One of them managed to deliver a blow to his chest that sprayed blood onto the beast's face, but Hades didn't so much as flinch. He beheaded the monster and kept going.

He was nearly to the end when he defeated the last attacker. Just twenty feet away. There was nothing between him and solid ground as the bridge swayed beneath his feet.

When a woman appeared at the other end of the bridge, I blinked.

She looked just like me.

She was slight, with her long dark hair whipping in the wind and too-large eyes dark with fear. She wore a simple white dress, and as I squinted to take in every inch of her, there was no question that she looked *exactly* like me.

For the first time since the challenge had begun, I saw Hades stiffen. He turned to look back at me and frowned, his gaze searching blindly. I waved my arms and shouted. "Hades! That's not me!"

He shook his head as if trying to fix his vision, then turned back to the other woman. She walked toward him, tears pouring down her face and her hand outstretched. She looked so desperate, so pleading, that even I wanted to go to her and help her.

It felt weird as hell.

She was nearly to him when she turned abruptly, appearing to stumble, then fell from the bridge.

I screamed, lunging forward. Even from here, I could see her small form pinwheeling through the air as she plummeted into the darkness below. In the flash of a second, Hades' golden wings had flared from his back.

"No!" I screamed, reaching out to stop him.

He *had* to make it across.

My throat burned as I yelled, "She's just an illusion!"

He didn't seem to hear me. It all happened so fast as he reached for the rope railing, clearly planning to throw himself over the edge and fly down to save her.

I reached out for him with my magic, trying to force him to feel me behind him, safe. Trying to force a connection that would break through the illusion that had worked so well on him.

When it happened, I felt it, like a wire connecting the two of us. He stiffened and turned back to me. His dark eyes still searched the area where I stood, and he clearly couldn't see me. But he didn't leap over after the fallen woman, either.

"Hades! Just go!" I screamed, praying he would hear me.

A great shudder racked his body, and he turned,

heading toward the other end, his stride picking up pace.

"Go, go," I found myself chanting, wanting him to reach the other side so that he could turn back and see that I was here and safe.

Finally, he set foot on solid ground. As soon as he did, he spun around and searched for me, his gaze finally landing. The tension that drained from his shoulders was so obvious that I could almost feel his relief.

His golden wings disappeared, and he nodded.

Why had that just happened? Was that a fear of his —losing me?

But of course. I was being naive. Of course he feared losing me. He needed me for his plan. Nothing more, nothing less. I needed to keep my head and not get soft.

I drew in a breath and faced the bridge.

My turn.

I swallowed hard and stepped onto the bridge before I could wimp out.

Please don't send any monsters at me.

I really didn't have the skill set to deal with that.

My heart thundered in my head as I took my first step, placing my foot carefully on the wooden slat as I white-knuckled the rope handrails. Below, the crevasse plunged thousands of feet into a deep mist below. My gut churned with a newfound fear of heights, and I went as quickly as I could, palms sweating as my knees trembled.

Every time the boards creaked underfoot, my skin went icy. I was halfway across when the rope handrail began to fray. Right under my grip, the fibers started to snap. Within seconds, the entire thing had broken through. With the tension gone, the right side of the bridge sagged.

I gasped and grabbed the left handrail rope with both hands, shuffling to line my feet up under the rail. The entire thing shuddered and pitched, and I looked wildly toward Hades.

He stared at me with his arms crossed, his brow set in concern. But he didn't look nearly as worried as I'd have expected.

I was about to *die* here.

And he appeared totally unfazed, as if he were watching me stroll across.

Maybe he couldn't see me?

But what did it matter? I didn't want him swooping to my rescue on golden wings. I had to pass this challenge myself. Take care of myself.

I drew in a shuddery breath as I began to inch my way across, hanging on to the rope rail with both hands as I shuffled my feet forward.

I can do this. I can do this.

Echo appeared at my head, fluttering along as he shot me encouraging glances. I was totally doing this. What was a little thing like a broken rope bridge over a crevasse into hell?

As if the universe could hear my thoughts, the rope rail that I clutched began to fray, the individual fibers snapping.

No.

It was going to break.

I had seconds.

I'd never survive the fall.

My magic flared to life, coming from deep within me. It was the only way out. I had to use it.

Frantic, I searched for any form of life in the crevasse below. Trees, bushes, vines—anything I could make grow up and catch me. Echo landed on my shoulder, and his magic surged into me, making mine stronger as it reached farther into the pit.

When I felt the life below, I nearly cried out in gratitude. Instead, I focused on it.

Grow. Grow.

I didn't know quite what it was, but it felt like a tree or other plant. They were my specialty, after all. Even though I could feel the life in animals, I couldn't control them.

Through my panic, a vision of a massive alligator rising up to save me flashed in my mind.

Nope!

I needed to focus.

The last of the rope threads snapped, leaving only the wobbly planks connected by their own crappy ropes. I dropped down to them, clinging like a monkey as the base of the rope bridge swayed in the wind. Below, the crevasse looked endless.

Without handrails, I couldn't walk upright.

Come on.

I could feel the vines growing, but not fast enough.

Come on.

On my left side, the rope that held the wooden slats together began to unravel, and I watched with horror as it finally snapped. The bridge dipped heavily to one side, connected to solid land by only one rope. I swung wildly, clinging to the last rope with my arms and legs wrapped around it and a few of the wooden slats that dangled in the breeze.

Just one rope left. It was no longer a bridge, just a terrifying collection of wood and rope.

Panic threatened to blank my mind, but I sucked in a deep breath. *Get it together, Seraphia.*

Suddenly, I could feel the plants more strongly, as if they were responding to my determination. I looked down and spotted a ragtag collection of foliage rising from the depths. Several thick vines, a couple of tree branches, and a weirdly tall bush reached toward me through the mist. I stretched out a hand, touching the rough bark of the branch. It shuddered and grew larger, and I climbed onto it.

The vines coiled under my legs, and the scrubby bush helped push me upright until I was all but walking on the greenery that had come to my rescue. Elation and power filled me as it carried me across the crevasse to safety.

I was nearly to Hades when his eyes widened with shock. "Seraphia?"

The plants set me down on the ground in front of Hades, and he stared at me, clearly confused. "You were just on the bridge. In the middle."

"It broke." I stepped forward on wobbly legs, then turned to the greenery that had saved me. I ran a grateful hand over the bush and smiled. "Thank you.'

The plants seemed to nod, then shrank back down into the crevasse. Echo was still on my shoulder, and he chattered his goodbye.

Heart racing, I turned to Hades. He was staring at me with confusion.

"You didn't see any of that, did you?" I asked.

"I saw you appear out of the mist riding on your foliage like a queen, but anything that came before that, no." He shook his head, concern in his eyes. "What happened?"

"Just a few problems with the bridge." I frowned, wondering if I'd seen the truth of his journey. "What happened when you crossed?"

He described it just as I'd seen it, and I frowned. "I wonder why it let me see you accurately, but it concealed me from you."

"I would have intervened if I'd known you were in trouble," he said.

Ah, of course. That newfound hyper-protectiveness of his. And he had wings, so he could have plucked me right out of the problem.

"Well, I can take care of myself," I said. The temple called to me now that I was close, and I wanted to get this over with. "Let's go."

I started forward. He followed, the lure for answers too great to resist.

The clouds overhead shifted ominously, moving far too quickly to be natural. They surrounded the temple, casting it in dark shadow.

"It almost feels as if the temple doesn't want us here," I said.

Hades looked up at the clouds. "It's just your imagination."

"Hmm." I doubted it. If this was a place of memory and fate, perhaps it knew what Hades intended and didn't want it to happen. The other gods certainly didn't want him to succeed.

I *definitely* didn't.

Still, I was here, and I was going to uphold my part of the bargain.

Together, we climbed the wide stairs to the front of the temple. There was no door, but rather a huge opening leading directly into the temple. Magic rolled out from the place, ancient and powerful. It vibrated through my limbs, and I straightened my spine.

I'd proven myself worthy. I wouldn't cower now.

Hades stuck close by my side as we walked into the middle of the temple. It was a massive, empty space tiled with wide slabs of marble. In the center of the temple, a narrow set of stairs led straight down into darkness.

"Are there attendants?" I asked Hades.

He shook his head. "No one living attends here. When one desires to meet with the keepers of memory, one must descend the stairs."

"And the freaking *Titans* are down there?" I shivered at the idea. They'd been the predecessors of the gods, enormous and powerful. If one of them took a dislike to me, I'd be in serious trouble.

"Just their spirits, held together by memory. Not the Titans themselves."

"So they can't hurt us."

"No. Not with their bodies, at least. Guard your mind against whoever visits you when you descend. It is most likely to be Coeus, the Titan of knowledge. He is purported to be even-tempered."

I clung to the thought. Even-tempered, I could deal with. Still, I eyed the stairs with trepidation. "And we're both supposed to go down there?"

He nodded. "One at a time."

"You first, then."

"All right."

I stepped back, watching him stride toward the stairwell. As he disappeared into the gloom, I held my breath.

19

HADES

Darkness enveloped me as I descended the stairs. Magic surged on the air, and I shuddered, reminded too much of my time in Tartarus. Perhaps it was the smell—death and decay—or the odd, hazy quality of the light. Whatever it was, I wanted to finish this as quickly as I could.

The faint glow from the temple gave just enough light that I could see the stairs in front of me. As the illumination from above faded, torches flickered to life along the walls. The golden glow revealed carvings scratched into the ancient stone, ornate depictions of gods and Titans as they ruled the earth.

The stairs appeared endless, seeming to go into the

depths of the rock, and I stopped, studying one of the carvings to my right. There was something almost familiar about it, though I knew I'd never seen it before. The lines dug into the stone formed a man of powerful proportions. As I stared at it, a dark mist seemed to rise up from the carving. I stepped back, frowning.

It took only seconds before the mist had formed a vaguely human-shaped figure. The being was semi-transparent, with no face that I could see, but enormous power radiated from it. It trembled through my bones, rare in its strength. The magic was dark and familiar, but I shook my head, trying to focus on what was in front of me.

"Are you Coeus?" I asked.

"I am not." The voice reverberated through the stairwell. It sounded vaguely like the voice of the darkness that spoke to me.

Could this be that same voice? It had never had form before, never been more than a shadowy sound and a feeling. It was the universe speaking to me, a power greater than myself.

Or was it?

"Who are you?" I asked.

The figure ignored the question, and my suspicion flared. Before I could demand again, it said, "The moment toward which you have been working will come tonight at midnight."

Shock lanced me. "Midnight? So quickly?"

"Everything has begun now. It will move quickly, or you will fail."

"I will *not* fail." Even the idea was anathema.

"Perhaps not. But you will face a great choice, Hades, Lord of the Underworld. If you choose incorrectly, eternal suffering will be yours."

"More Tartarus." I already knew that.

"*Eternal* Tartarus. This is your only chance to change your fate. If you do not choose correctly, you will never return to your realm. Instead, you will be a prisoner of Tartarus forever."

My heart pounded. *That* was new. At worst, I'd thought I'd be sent back to Tartarus for another round of torture. But those rounds were temporary. Terrible, but temporary.

What this Titan was suggesting was not.

How had I never learned this before? And what could possibly turn me from my chosen path?

Nothing.

The figure drifted back toward the wall, and suddenly, I was alone.

"Tell me who you are," I demanded of the silence. There was something here that I wasn't understanding. Or perhaps, that I didn't *want* to understand.

Confusion tore at me, along with the strangest sense of betrayal and anger.

But I could not turn away from the things I did not want to face. I needed to know.

He was gone, however, and magic dragged me from the stairwell back up to the temple. One moment I was on the stairs, the next, I was in the temple next to Seraphia.

"Well?" She stepped forward, eyes wide with curiosity.

She was such a welcome change from the darkness in the pit. I wanted to pull her into my arms and bury my face in her hair.

I clenched my fists, determined not to give in to my weakness. Instead, I drew in a ragged breath and said, "I have finished. You may go down."

She frowned at me. "It didn't take long."

"No. But do not be afraid."

She scowled at me. "I'm not afraid."

I nodded, not knowing what to say. My head was spinning with what I'd just seen. With what might be true.

"I'll be back." Seraphia turned away from me and descended. I watched her disappear, my heart thundering.

Fear for her shot through me, horrible and acid.

I'd spent nearly my entire existence without ever feeling fear. Dread and misery, yes, but never fear. Not even of Tartarus.

And yet, when she walked into danger, all I felt was the sickening spread of fear.

Breathing hard, I stood at the top of the stairs, looking down into the gloom, trying my best to hear any movement from her.

We were nearing my end goal—what I'd worked so long for—and the strangest sense of doubt was beginning to creep in.

The light.

I could blame the light and what we'd done last night. It had poisoned me, brought me over to her side. I ground my teeth, clenching a fist as I tried to regain control of myself.

This lack of focus was unacceptable. There was only one option ahead of me. I could not falter.

Seraphia

My skin prickled with nerves as I descended the stairs. The shadows grew deeper, enveloping me. When it had become so dark that the stairs had nearly disappeared in front of me, torches flared to life on either side. More torches gleamed against the walls below, disappearing into the depths of the earth.

I shivered.

How deep did it go? To the center of the world, it looked like.

I drew in a deep breath and kept going, my mind spinning with possibilities of what I would find down there. I was so distracted that I stumbled. Breath caught, I reached out to stabilize myself and grasped the wall.

My fingertips dipped into a divot, and I looked over, frowning.

There was a carving on the wall: a man, tall and broad. As I watched, a dark mist crept from the stone. I stumbled backward, and within seconds, a figure stood before me. His body was formed entirely of the mist that had seeped from the wall, as if I'd ignited a spell just by touching it. Even though the creature stood on the stairs below me, he was still taller than I was.

Was it even a man? I had no idea.

The magic that billowed from it nearly bowled me over, and I stepped backward a few steps, climbing away from the figure. Its magic smelled of decay and tasted like rotten fruit. My heart thundered in my ears as I breathed shallowly, trying to absorb as little of the magic as possible.

Despite the disgusting nature of it, the darkness inside me seemed to respond positively, rising up inside me. From nowhere, Echo landed on my shoulder. I clung to him, drawing strength.

"Persephone." The voice rumbled through me, and I shuddered.

I didn't bother correcting the figure. Instead, I just stared hard at it. "Why am I here?"

"To fulfill your destiny at Akamas."

"Akamas?" I hadn't heard the name of that place in years. I was *from* Arcadia. It was a tiny village on Cyprus where I'd been born.

"Yes. The plain by the sea. That is where your destiny will fulfill itself."

"*That* is the place from my vision?" I hadn't recognized it.

"Yes."

Fates, had it been so long since I'd seen that plain that I hadn't even noticed it was my home?

Yes.

I'd left so long ago, I hardly remembered anything. But how could this figure know so much? "Who are you?" I shivered. "You feel a bit like the darkness in the pit beneath Hades' castle."

The figure merely inclined its head at that statement and said, "I am Chronos."

Chronos? Hades' *father*?

Holy fates, did Hades know that? If so, he'd never mentioned it.

But was Chronos really his father? The myths said so, but they weren't right about me.

"Shouldn't you be in Tartarus?" I asked.

"Indeed, I should. And I am. For now."

"For now?"

The words made a chill race over my skin. Worse, I still felt the darkness rising inside me, drawn by his proximity. It was like he called it out of me, trying to get it to take over my soul.

"You will do as your destiny commands, Persephone." The voice rumbled through me, tugging at the darkness.

I resisted, stepping back onto the stair behind me. I needed to get the hell out of here. I'd fulfilled my part of the bargain and walked into this stupid stairwell, and now it was time to go.

"You cannot run from it," he said. "You will not want to." He waved a hand in front of his face, and an image appeared.

My three friends—Eve, Mac, and Beatrix—all bound in black rope, their eyes wide.

"What did you do?" I demanded, rage and fear rising within me.

"Incentive." Satisfaction rumbled through the voice. "I know that you resist your fate, and I am helping it along."

My anger bubbled to the surface, surging through me as I fought the fear that threatened to drown me.

"You do not like this?" the monster asked. "What about this?" He flicked a hand, and Beatrix screamed, her face twisted in pain. "I can do that as much as I like."

Fury like I'd never known filled me to boiling, turning my soul black and my intentions blacker. I reached out toward the shadowy figure, vines sprouting from my hands, though I held no plants. They wrapped around Chronos, finding purchase despite the fact that he appeared incorporeal. They squeezed tightly, and satisfaction surged through me. I'd make him pay for what he'd done to my friends.

Tighter.

I commanded the vines with my mind, and they obeyed, wrapping around him in such great quantity that he nearly disappeared under their weight. The image in front of him flickered away, and all I could see was my handwork.

The darkness within me rejoiced, rising stronger as I tried to squeeze the life from him. It was a heady feeling, all this power and control. Vengeance.

But in the flash of an eye, he dematerialized from within the vines and appeared outside of their grasp, standing on the stair closer to me.

Shock lanced me as I stared at him, my soul still screaming for me to attack him. Destroy him.

"You liked that, didn't you?" he asked.

His words disgusted me. His tone, too. I stumbled backward, not even recognizing myself.

I hadn't really been helping my friends when I'd attacked him. They weren't even here. Yet I'd still attacked, pointlessly fueled by rage. Fueled by the darkness.

I was growing weaker. Succumbing even more easily.

I shook my head, frantically trying to clear my thoughts. It only kind of worked. Terrified for my friends, I looked at him. "Where are they?"

"Akamas."

"How do I know you really have them?"

"Does it matter?"

No. Just the threat was enough. I had to check.

"Hurry, and you might find them alive."

I spun on my heel and ran, racing up the stairs as my heart pounded wildly in my ears. *He'd kidnapped them.*

Fear chilled my skin as I raced up into the main temple, nearly plowing into Hades. He gripped my arms and stared down at me, concern creasing his brow. "Are you all right?"

Gasping, I looked back behind me. Chronos had not followed me up, but his threats had.

"Come on." I grabbed Hades' hand and pulled him toward the exit. "We've got to go."

"Did you get the location?" he demanded, not moving.

"Yes." I yanked him hard, glowering. "Now come on, he's got my friends."

He followed, hand gripping mine tightly. "Your friends? What do you mean?"

"I mean that he has kidnapped them." I sprinted

down the temple stairs and toward the river. The dark water snaked through the fields. "Call Charon. We need to go to Guild City."

In the back of my mind, I knew I was being manipulated. But I couldn't take the risk. What if he really had them?

I searched the sky, hoping to see Beatrix flying among the gray clouds.

I didn't, of course.

"You're going to have to explain," Hades said.

"I will, as soon as you call Charon with the boat."

He nodded. "He's already coming. He will be here soon."

Anxious, I stared out at the water. We needed to get a move on. Finally, I spotted Charon in the distance. He must not have been far away. Satisfied that he was coming, I looked up at Hades and explained what the shadowy figure had told me, finishing with, "Is he really capable of kidnapping my friends?"

Hades frowned. "Presumably. But you say that the figure was Chronos?"

"Yes. Why do you look shocked?"

"I saw him as well, but he did not give me a name."

I frowned at him. There was more to this than he was saying. "He's the same voice as the one in the pit beneath your castle."

"I think you are correct."

"Did you not know that before?" I asked.

"The voice never had a name until now. It certainly never had a form. I didn't know if I was listening to the voice of the universe itself, or if it had come from my own imagination." He shook his head. "For millennia, that was enough to explain it. Then you arrived, and I began to question it. When you fell into the pit, I started to suspect that all was not as it seemed."

I recalled the power in the voice from the pit—the strength and comfort. It was all Hades had ever known. I couldn't imagine it. No wonder he'd turned out the way he had, if that was the closest thing he had to a parent.

"Not as it seemed?" I asked.

"Perhaps it *is* Chronos."

"Does that change things for you?"

He face hardened slightly. "My goals are the same as they have ever been, if that is what you are asking."

I scowled at him. "That is what I'm asking."

Finally, Charon pulled up alongside us, his ragged robes fluttering in the faint wind. He held out a skeletal hand, and Hades gave him two coins, then helped me into the boat. Normally, I might dodge away and try to do it myself, but I was reeling so hard from everything I'd learned that I appreciated the assistance.

Once we were seated, Charon moved to the bow and plunged his stick into the dark water, dragging us away from the temple. I looked back, a shiver racing over my skin. I met Hades' gaze, then nodded toward Charon. "Can he hear us?"

Hades waved a hand in front of us, and magic sparked on the air. "Not anymore."

I turned to him, drawing in a deep breath to ask the question he probably wouldn't like. "Is Chronos your father?"

20

*H*ADES

Was Chronos my father?

I frowned, staring down at Seraphia. "I do not know."

"Really?"

I shook my head. "I was never a child, so there was no need for me to meet whatever made me. From what I know, I was born of the darkness."

"I saw. But Chronos *was* the darkness when I saw him."

"I've never seen him in Tartarus," I said. "But I knew he was there."

Surprise flashed in her eyes. "You've been?"

I debated what to tell her, torn. Finally, I nodded jerkily.

She frowned. "I thought it was only for Titans."

"And for me."

"How so?"

I stared out at the scenery passing by. We were nearly there. I just needed to distract her for a bit until then. "He has your friends?"

Worry flashed on her face again.

My comment had worked to distract her, but guilt followed.

What the hell? I rubbed my chest, strangely uncomfortable with the feeling.

"Could he really kidnap them?" It was the second time she'd asked. It had to be a nervous tic, because she was far too smart to have forgotten.

"Yes." If the darkness that compelled me really was Chronos—which seemed possible—it could be capable of kidnapping. Using her friends as bait was something I would have done.

It certainly complicated matters if the darkness were Chronos, as I now believed. I'd have to deal with that. He couldn't be allowed to escape Tartarus, if that was his goal. I would stop him.

I looked at Seraphia, and the sight of her pale, frightened face made something twist in my chest. *Hard.*

She hugged herself, staring at the water, fear in her

eyes. I could feel her misery from here, even though we didn't touch.

Helplessness clawed at me. Seeing her like this was strangely uncomfortable for me. I certainly didn't like it. I wanted to fix this for her.

But how?

Suddenly, I wanted to distract her. I wanted to tell her what drove me. When I'd first met her, I hadn't cared at all what she thought. Now, I felt compelled to share with her. I wanted her to understand my actions.

It was the strangest thing.

"Tartarus was built for Titans," I could hear myself saying. "But once a millennium, they make room for me."

Her eyes flashed toward me, surprised. "What?"

I nodded, staring out at the river. "My goal—to spread the realm of the underworld to earth—has been imprinted upon me since my creation long ago. But every thousand years, if I have not succeeded, I am taken to Tartarus to remind me of my goals."

"Remind you?"

"You've seen my back."

"Torture."

I nodded. "The only kind of torture that can permanently mark a god. It takes a while, of course. It is... unpleasant." An understatement.

She swallowed, her face even paler than it had been. "I had no idea."

"Why would you?"

She just shook her head, clearly shocked, and leaned against me. Her warmth blazed into me, and I drew on it, taking strength.

"Is it almost the thousand-year mark?" she asked.

I nodded and drew off one of my gloves, revealing my hand. It flickered, turning slightly transparent, and she gasped.

"This is the beginning," I said.

"Damn it."

I frowned at her.

She shook her head, staring forward and muttering, "So many to save."

I gripped her hand. "Don't think that way."

She looked up at me. "Of course I think that way."

"Your friends will be fine."

"It's not just my friends."

"Then who else?" She hadn't mentioned anyone else when coming out of the stairwell.

"*You*, you idiot."

Shock lanced me, so fierce and sharp that it left me stunned.

She looked away, staring out at the water. "Can't Charon go any faster?"

Finally, I found my words. "You want to...save me?"

"I didn't." She wouldn't look at me. "But now, I don't know. Your goals are still the same, and I can't let you achieve them. But still..."

"Don't. You don't need to save me." I didn't like the idea of it. Nor did I like the warmth that tried to fill me when I thought of her wanting to try. "There's nothing to save me from."

She laughed and looked down at my hand. "Sure."

"This is my destiny. I choose it."

"You've known nothing else. How can you choose something when you have only one option? That's not choice."

Fates, what was happening here?

She shook her head. "Actually, I'm wrong. You didn't start out having a choice. But you have one now, because I've felt the light in you."

Her words were an unwelcome reminder, as was the feeling of that same light. It almost seemed to respond to the things she was saying.

I couldn't afford that. Not now.

I needed to be victorious in this—to stay on my path. More than that, I needed to ensure she was on that same path with me. She was almost there. Chronos threatening her friends had helped.

Finally, Charon landed on the bank near the entrance to my realm. Seraphia scrambled off and waited for me, her expression impatient. I climbed from the boat, and Charon moved away from the shore, drifting back toward his duties.

"Let's go." Seraphia waved her hand. "Call on the horses."

I nodded and called upon my magic. The horses appeared a moment later, and I helped her mount Styx.

She nudged the animal in the sides and took off toward the gate toward my territory. I leapt onto Horse and followed, quickly catching up.

Seraphia

Sally seemed to sense my anxiety, because she hotfooted it toward the gate. Hades kept pace easily, and we whipped by Cerberus. I wanted to stop to greet the dog, but there was no time. Echo squeaked as he flew past the giant hound, and I had to assume it was a quick farewell.

As we thundered through the forest on our mounts, I couldn't stop thinking of the vision of my friends. Was Chronos torturing them even now?

The idea made rage swell inside me. It was preferable to fear, and I clung to it, letting it drive me harder, faster. The forest whipped by, dark and nearly dead, and I didn't spare much more than a glance for it as I bent low over Sally's neck and hung on tight.

The farther we rode, the angrier I grew. I felt it twisting inside me until it was all I could think of. Though I knew this was Cronos's attempt to get me where he wanted me, I couldn't help but follow along. Of *course* I had to immediately find out if my friends were really trapped.

We exited the forest and reached the plain, riding toward the sea. The waves crashed against the cliffs below, but I had eyes only for the city on the hill. Nearly there.

Hades kept close by my side as we ascended the hill. Near the main tower that housed the wooden gate, Sally slowed. I tried to nudge her on, but she wouldn't go. He'd stopped her using his magic.

"You're going to plow right into the gate," Hades said.

I gritted my teeth and stared at it, my lungs heaving. "This is what you wanted, right? Me heading hellbent toward doomsday?"

"Yes, but I want you arriving in one piece."

It was true enough that I couldn't do much to help my friends if I had a broken neck, but it was hard to slow down. It felt like the hounds of hell were nipping at my heels.

Finally, the gate in front of us opened.

Hades looked at me, frowning. "A moment."

He waved a hand at me, and the clothes that I wore changed. I gasped, looking down at the dark cloak and fine dress of thick black silk. There was a faint weight on my head, and I knew without looking that there would be a crown there—probably similar to the one that Hades now wore.

We were entering the city, where we would see his subjects.

"Why?" I asked, still looking down at myself.

"You will be my queen."

The words sent something shivering through me, horror and delight all at once. I didn't want to rule hell by his side. But he no doubt thought I was going to, since I was currently headed right toward everything he wanted me to do.

"I can't think about that right now." I nudged Sally, determined to ignore Hades and my new clothes. They didn't matter if I wanted to be quick about saving my friends.

Sally trotted through the gates, Hades and Horse to the left.

As expected, people drifted out of their houses, gazing in awe at us. This was the first time they'd seen me dressed as a queen, and they clearly didn't care that it was little more than clothing. The reverence in their eyes shot straight into the dark heart of me, making something shiver and grow.

I frowned.

That wasn't me. I'd never liked attention much, and this was the most intense kind of attention. But I liked it now, *way* too much. The darkness inside me seemed to purr, reveling in their awe, in the power that it implied.

That was all the damned darkness wanted—*power*. Too bad for me that it felt so damned good. It drove away my doubts and fears and made me feel confident and strong. It was so hard to resist.

I drew in a ragged breath, determined to succeed. I diverted my gaze from them, keeping it high over their heads as I stared at the massive library in front of us. We were nearly to the portal that would take me back to Guild City, and from there, to my friends.

I couldn't help but take a peek at Hades, however. He looked regal and powerful as always in his black armor and golden crown. But it was the pride in his eyes when he looked at me that made me unable to look away.

Something had changed in him.

I'd felt it before. I could see it even now.

The light was growing.

Did he feel it? Did he fight it, like I fought the dark?

I shook my head, trying to drive away the thought. I needed to focus on my friends. They needed me.

We neared the library steps a few moments later, and I bounded off Sally. The dress and cloak that wrapped around my legs nearly tripped me, but I managed to keep my footing. Hades was at my side in a second, and he followed me up the stairs.

"This dress is stupid," I muttered, holding up piles of it in my hands so that I could run.

"You are right." He flicked a hand, and the dress changed into dark, tight trousers. My top was still the bodice of the dress, dark and magnificent as it swept low to bare my shoulders and tight down my arms. There were plates of metal sewn into it, beautiful but hard—armor of some sort. The cloak still swept from my shoulders, and I realized that I was dressed as I had been in my vision when I'd walked from the underworld onto the earth with Hades at my side.

The vision is coming true.

It was enough to chill my blood.

No.

I was in control. I wouldn't give in.

Heart pounding, I ascended the last steps. Hades reached forward and opened the massive library door, not needing a key. I stepped inside the cavernous space, ignoring the magnificent soaring ceilings and the spiders lurking in their webs, watching me.

Quickly, I hurried toward the portal, lunging inside and letting the ether suck me in. The underworld pulled on me, a tearing pain from the pomegranate potion. I ignored it.

When the ether spit me out in my library, I stumbled forward, clutching my chest. The pomegranate potion still hurt like hell. Hades arrived only a half second behind me. I turned to him. "Can you leave the library now?"

"With you at my side, yes. We are fulfilling the ancient prophecy to spread the darkness, which makes it possible."

I swallowed hard, remembering the vision I'd had. This was it exactly, down to my clothes.

I shook away my fear. I'd deal with it. "Let's go."

Together, we strode through the library. The stacks towered on either side, warm golden wood lit by the flickering flame of the candles that floated in the air.

When I stepped out into the dim light of dusk, Hades followed. I turned to him, taking in his tall form. The crown was gone, but his long cloak, the armor, and his regal bearing made him stand out like a sore thumb. Guild City was used to the magical, but it wasn't used to *gods.* Certainly not gods who dressed like warriors of old and looked like they could tear the place apart with their bare hands.

His form flickered, turning transparent, and I gasped. "What's happened to you?"

He looked down at his arm and frowned. "It is the curse. It's stronger when I walk upon the earth. I don't have long."

Holy fates. "You'll be dragged to Tartarus if I don't do what you need me to?" He nodded sharply, and I wanted to scream. "Why didn't you tell me that earlier?"

"It wasn't necessary."

It sure as hell felt necessary now. I was only going to go rescue my friends, not spread the darkness from the underworld to earth. I'd thought there was nothing that could make me do that.

And there *was* nothing. No matter how much I was growing to care for Hades, I couldn't do that. Not even to save him.

I bit back the sob that tried to climb out of my throat and turned away from him to head down the street. I had barely made it half a step when he reached for my arm and pulled me back. His eyes burned into mine as he said, "We will find your friends and save them. I vow it."

I swallowed hard. I shouldn't want the words. I shouldn't need them.

I *could* save them myself.

But having him offer to help—to vow it—definitely twisted something inside my chest. Especially considering that he was facing his own destruction. He thought of me.

I pressed my lips together and nodded, my eyes pricking with tears. "Thanks." I turned away, then stopped, looking back. I hated to ask, but I had to know. The stakes were so high for him, after all. "Did you plan this?"

The shock in his eyes couldn't be faked. Hell, unless we were naked together, I never saw such emotion in him. Finally, he shook his head. "I did not."

The honesty satisfied me, as did the memory of him being genuinely surprised that Chronos might be the voice in the abyss around which his entire existence revolved.

There was more going on here than either of us understood, but we were about to get to the bottom of it.

"Come on." I whirled around and strode through the town, barely noticing the strange glances we got.

In human London, we'd have looked like we were going to a fancy party. In Guild City, the citizens knew enough to think we were strange and best avoided. Not a single person stayed on our side of the street as we strode forward.

"You're making quite an impression," I muttered to Hades as we raced along.

"I'm not sure it's me."

"What?" I turned to him, then caught sight of my reflection in a shop window.

Holy fates, I looked insane. My eyes blazed with green fire, and my skin glowed with light. Scarlet painted my lips, so red it could have been blood.

I am a goddess.

Apparently, something about the last few hours had changed me. Maybe my sense of purpose, or the darkness that was even now threatening to overwhelm me. The fear for my friends fed it and kept it going.

Next to me, Hades looked like the king he was, striding along as his midnight cloak whipped behind him.

We reached the alley that led to the Shadow Guild tower a moment later, and I could feel Hades' confusion. I didn't bother explaining, just raced down the narrow passage and out into the square in front of our tower.

The door hung open, the windows smashed.

I swallowed hard, horror racing through me, and sprinted up to the door. "Eve! Beatrix! Mac!"

Of course, there was no response, and I only needed to poke my head in to know that it was empty.

"We must go to wherever he has taken them," Hades said. "They're already there."

I gritted my teeth, anger rippling through me. "We need a transport charm first."

"I can teleport."

"Do you know where we are going?"

"No. Only you know that."

"Then give me a moment." I wasn't going to tell him where we were going, and the transport charms would give me more control. I raced into the main room and up the stairs, headed to Eve's workshop. It had been ransacked, and the sight of it made my anger even brighter. I managed to find a couple of transport charms near the broken shelf where she stored them, and I shoved them in my pocket.

I returned to Hades' side and set off toward the town exit.

"Where are you going?" he asked.

"We need to get to human London first. The gate is this way."

He nodded and followed. Together, we raced toward the main exit that led out of Guild City. The tower loomed high overhead, and we entered the narrow passage meant for foot traffic. The tunnel was dark and empty, and I hurried toward the portal at the other end.

As I neared, Hades gripped my hand. I clutched his in return, and we stepped into the portal. The ether swept us up and spat us out in the back hall of the Haunted Hound, the pub where Mac worked.

I let go of Hades' hand and hurried out into the main part of the pub. To my surprise, the seats weren't full of cozy patrons sipping pints. Instead, the place was empty save for Quinn, Carrow, and the Devil of Darkvale, all of whom stood by the bar. My only friends who *hadn't* been abducted.

I hurried over, searching their pale faces. "You know," I said.

They turned to me, shocked, their gazes going from my clothing to Hades.

Carrow, her wild golden hair messy from dragging her hands through it, gave me a quick hug. "I'm glad you're back." She pulled away and turned toward Hades, poking a finger into his chest. "Is this your fault?"

He frowned briefly, then said, "In a distant way, I'm sure it is. Not directly though, no."

She glared at him and stepped back, sizing him up. He absolutely towered over her, but she didn't cower. Carrow was our guild leader, and she was made of steel.

Behind her stood the Devil of Darkvale, Guild City's resident mob boss and the most powerful vampire in town. Hell, the most powerful supernatural in town, until Hades showed up. He was dressed impeccably as usual, though he'd given up his three-piece suit for simple, sturdy black clothes that I knew meant he planned to help Carrow find our missing friends. He studied Hades, his expression calm and cold. I'd always called him the Ice Man. He said nothing as he stared. Though Hades' form had been flickering earlier, he was solid now. Hopefully, it stayed that way.

"You're the one who abducted our Seraphia," Quinn said. The shifter crossed his big arms over his chest and glared at Hades. "You're not welcome here."

"On earth or in this establishment?" Hades looked around, slight curiosity in his gaze. He'd probably never seen a proper pub.

"Either," Quinn said.

Hades merely nodded, as if this were expected, and met my gaze. "Shall we go?"

"Where to?" Carrow demanded. "Do you know where they are?"

My fist clenched. "I have an idea."

21

Seraphia

It was obvious that Hades and my friends had no idea how to talk to each other. Fortunately, no one tried. We were all to focused on the goal at hand.

"Where are we going?" Carrow demanded as Quinn locked up the Haunted Hound.

"To Cyprus."

"Where you were born?"

I nodded. "This all has to do with me." A shiver of guilt ran through me. "It's my fault, really."

"It's not." She squeezed my arm. "Now, tell me what to expect."

"I have no idea." I looked at Hades. "Do you?"

He shook his head. "No more than you do."

Shit. I looked at Carrow, Quinn, and the Devil. "We're going to a field. I think. Somehow, I'm supposed to spread the darkness of the underworld to earth. At least, that's what the kidnapper wants me to do."

"I assume that's not actually on your agenda?" Carrow asked.

"No." I hiked a thumb at Hades. "It's on his, though."

Hades just stared at them. He really wasn't the best with people. Didn't care what they thought, and it showed. It had never been so obvious that he was on a godly plane and everyone else on a mortal one.

"We won't be letting that happen," the Devil said. They were the only words he spoke, and his tone was so cold that it could give Antarctica a run for its money.

Hades just stared at him but said nothing. He didn't need to prove anything to strangers. Unfortunately, the silence of his utter confidence was unnerving.

"We're going to go and save them," I said. "From what, exactly, I do not know."

"There was a report of a dark shadow, and that was it," Carrow said.

I nodded. "That tracks, given what I've seen."

"Well, you deal with it, and we'll save them," Carrow said. "Just let us know if you need any other backup."

"Deal." I handed her a transport charm. "We'll go to the same beach we went to last time, all right? It's near where I think they're being held."

She took the charm and nodded. "I know where it is."

It hadn't been more than a couple months since we'd gone to Cyprus to sort out a problem she'd had. Fortunately, she knew enough about the location to get herself there, which would make things quicker.

Hades looked down at me. "Now?"

I nodded, struck anew by how out of place he was here.

He gripped my hand, and I didn't fight it, just held on tight. It was all so screwed up between us—our goals, our feelings, all of it. But still, his touch was comforting.

I reached into my pocket and withdrew the transport charm, then threw it to the ground. It exploded upward in a poof of glittering silver smoke. A few yards away, Carrow threw hers to the ground as well.

Hades and I stepped into our portal. Carrow entered hers with Quinn and the Devil of Darkvale. The ether spun me through space, but Hades held on tight. A few moments later, it spat us out on the rocky shoreline of Cyprus.

Moonlight glittered on the waves, illuminating the hills around me. Next to me, Hades' form flickered. Fear stabbed me.

If he disappeared, he'd be gone.

I don't want him to be gone. The deepest grief gripped my chest, so strange and unexpected, yet also unsurprising.

I've fallen for him.

And he might not make it.

He held out his hand. "Give me the potion your friend Eve made you. The one that will allow you to leave the underworld."

My jaw slackened. "You're going to give your approval?"

"If you do as I ask, yes."

My brow lowered. "And you ask that I spread the darkness to the earth."

"It is the same as it always has been."

Disgusted, I dug the vial out of my pocket and shoved it at him. Frankly, I was grateful to find it there, given that he'd done a magical costume change on me.

Of course, I wasn't going to spread the darkness, but there was no point in holding onto the vial. Maybe he would change his mind.

I turned from him, looking for Carrow, Quinn, and the Devil. They stood a dozen yards away, and I caught Carrow's eye as I pointed up the hill to my right. She nodded, and we all began to climb.

"How far away are we?" Hades asked.

"If I remember correctly, there is a field near here. It's the one that Chronos told me about. There should be some trees and boulders to hide behind so we can scout it out."

He nodded, keeping close by our side. Our small group moved silently up the hillside, and the entire place felt oddly empty. The sea breeze blew my hair into my face, and I shoved it back, using the bright moonlight to guide my way.

"There's no one here that I can sense," Hades murmured.

"Same." It was weird enough to send a shiver of nerves up my spine. Shouldn't I be able to feel my kidnapped friends' life forces?

Finally, we reached the edge of the field that I remembered vaguely from my childhood. I couldn't believe I hadn't recognized it. But then, why would I? I'd hardly ever come here.

Hades and I stayed behind the cover of a large boulder while the other three stuck to the trees nearby. I peeked around to see if I could spot my friends or their abductors. Almost immediately, I spotted three bodies lying prone in the middle of the field.

They were alone.

My heart leapt into my throat, nearly strangling me. I lunged out from behind the boulder.

Hades grabbed my arm, trying to yank me back. "It may not be safe."

"I don't care!" I tore free and raced forward.

There was no one else there. I'd have felt their life force.

I fell to my knees at the side of the first body. Mac. A sob tore from my throat. She lay so still and pale. Dead.

Carrow landed next to me, and her voice was strangled when she spoke. "Why them?" Frantically, she looked around. "Where are they? Who did this?"

"Gone." The dark mist wasn't here. Chronos wasn't here. I'd have felt him, and I didn't. Whoever had taken them had killed them and tossed them here.

My heart twisted, and tears blurred my eyes as I crawled over to Beatrix, spotting immediately that she was as still and cold and Mac. The same for Eve. Each of my beautiful friends, laid out like they were at their funerals. I drew in a ragged sob.

At some point, Hades appeared. It might have been seconds or hours.

His soft voice cut through my grief. "There's the faintest bit of life left in them."

"What?" Shock lanced me. I felt nothing coming from them.

Hades raised Mac's limp wrist, his fingertips pressed to her pulse. "It's very faint, but it's there."

"They sound dead." Carrow had her head pressed to Eve's chest, clearly listening for a heartbeat.

I reached for Mac's wrist and tried to feel a heart-beat. "I feel nothing."

"Death has not fully taken them," Hades said. "I would know."

He would. But if they weren't fully dead...

My mind raced as I frantically tried to figure out what the hell was going on. Only sort of dead? I could work with that. Just like I had back in the forest in the underworld. Those trees had been sort of dead, too.

Until you'd commanded them to suck the life from bunnies.

That was true, and bad, but this would be the other way around. A little grass and a few trees to bring back my friends was a worthy trade. We lit fires all the time to keep from freezing to death, so how was this any different?

But it was exactly like my vision.

I shuddered, trying to drive away the thought. Yes, on the surface, it was. But in my vision, I hadn't had my friends at my feet. I'd done it because I'd wanted to.

Except I *didn't* want to. And that would keep me from going too far.

All the same, we needed to be safe.

I looked up at Carrow. "I'm going to try something. But you need to be ready to get the hell out of here when they are well again. I don't know what's going to happen, and you could all be vulnerable." And I'd need to know exactly when I could stop taking the life from the earth. Too much, and I would lose myself. As soon as I knew they were well and safely away from here, I could stop.

Carrow nodded, gripping my arm. "You've got this."

Quinn caught my gaze. "We believe in you."

I nodded, grateful. I just wished I believed in me, too.

Instead, I was scared out of my wits.

Hades just watched me, still and silent. His form flickered briefly, going entirely transparent, and that same fear pierced me. He didn't have long, and I had no idea how to save him.

I tore my gaze away from him and rose. My legs shook as I walked away from my friends. If the darkness started to rise in me, I didn't want to be too close to them.

Heart pounding, I sank to my knees in the grass. My fingertips tingled as I reached for it, sinking them into the rough, prickly stuff. Cyprus had different grass than the soft, wet vegetation of England, and it felt like my childhood.

I could feel the life force beating through the slender stalks, pulsing from the tree trunks nearby.

Give.

I reached for the magic inside me, using it to call upon the life force in the earth. It came easily, my practice paying off. Too easily. I could feel Hades' gaze on me, and I both loved and loathed it.

As I watched, the grass began to wilt. Just like in my vision.

I'm doing this.

I shuddered and shoved the thought away, focusing on directing the life force into my friends. Every second that passed was agony as I waited to see if it would work. Worse, I could feel the darkness rising in me as I tried to manipulate the fabric of life to suit my own needs.

The power of it sang through my veins. As it began to work, I felt it. There was a feeling of being connected to everything—the grass, the trees, the animals, and the other people on the plain. The life between us was like energy, and I moved it around according to my will.

The tattoo on my arm glowed so brightly that it nearly blinded me. The power was staggering, making my head spin and my limbs tremble.

This was what it felt like to be a god?

Soon, I couldn't stop. I could feel my friends growing healthier, but I thought about them less and less. I just didn't care as much. All I could think of was the life that I sucked from the earth. Somehow, the darkness within me had bubbled up to the surface, taking control of my actions.

Yes.

"It's working!" Carrow whispered. "Keep going!"

I could feel it, and excitement rose inside me. My friends were growing stronger.

I took more from the earth, withering the grass, and then the trees. Every second that passed made me feel more powerful, more invincible. It was almost like being drunk.

Out of the corner of my vision, I caught sight of Carrow, Quinn, and the Devil helping our friends to their feet. They looked wobbly and pale, but fine enough.

"Seraphia?" Mac's voice filtered through the night.

"What happened?" Eve mumbled.

"I feel a bit odd," said Beatrix.

"It's done!" Carrow shouted. "You can stop, Seraphia."

"Get them out of here," I gasped.

Carrow nodded, and almost immediately, the six of them disappeared.

It was just me and Hades, and my gaze was drawn to him. His form disappeared briefly, and that same fear fought its way through the strange greed that ate at me.

Not Hades.

I didn't want to lose him, even if I didn't really have him.

The life in the earth.

If it had saved my friends, maybe it would save him, too. Going to Tartarus was like death. Perhaps I could make him strong enough to resist it. Even if it was only temporary, it would buy him time.

I fed my power into the earth, taking more and more. Giving it to Hades, but also keeping it for myself.

"What's happening?" Hades' voice carried over the roar in my head.

"Fixing you," I gasped.

He looked down at his arms, his brow creased.

Was it working?

It felt like it was working. So I kept going, feeding more life into him, trying to save him. The power made me feel like nothing could stop me. Distantly, I realized that it was like a poison, changing how I behaved.

I was going too far, but I couldn't stop.

I'm not strong enough.

Something deep within me urged me to keep going, and I did.

A massive cracking noise rent the night air, and the earth opened up in front of me. A great chasm appeared, dark smoke and mist billowing out.

Chronos.

Somehow, I knew it was him.

This had been the end goal all along, and I'd just ushered in the apocalypse.

No. I couldn't let it end here. The shock of what I'd done snapped some sense into me, dragging my real self to the surface. Horrified, I looked around. I knelt in the middle of a wasteland, all of the greenery dead as far as the eye could see. And in front of me, the earth formed a massive crevasse deep into the depths of evil.

The same darkness that resided in Hades' castle was rising to the surface.

Panic burst forth within me.

I couldn't release this onto the earth.

It would destroy everything.

I'd gone too far, and it didn't matter that I'd been trying to save those I loved.

I needed to knit the earth back together. Trap it.

But how?

Your life.

It came to me with blazing clarity. I needed to repair the earth, and the only thing that could do that would be to give it the life force it needed to recover. *My* life force.

Fear roared through me, but determination pushed me on. I had to fix this. As I had at the forest, I pushed my life force into the earth, trying to reverse what I had done. Instead of taking, I gave.

I looked over at Hades, who appeared to be fully corporeal again. I couldn't truly tell if it had worked, but I wanted to believe it had.

Weakness tugged at me as I worked, my head going woozy. I could feel the earth repairing itself just as I could feel the darkness still rising. It came from far away, and I still had time.

Please let me have time.

Tears rolled down my cheeks, and my muscles ached. Echo landed on my shoulder, lending his strength to mine. But it wasn't enough. When my vision began to fade, I knew.

I wouldn't survive this.

22

HADES

What was going on?

Everything felt different.

My body, for one. Seraphia had clearly done something to me, feeding the life of the earth into my body, healing me. I could still feel the curse that would drag me back to Tartarus, but it was far weaker than it had ever been.

She'd staved it off somehow.

And yet, she looked drained. She knelt in the moonlight, her shoulders bowed as her right hand gripped the dead grass at her knees. Her skin was ghostly pale, and her magic seemed to be flowing out of her. All around, the dying earth was reviving.

She was undoing her work.

Why?

I stepped up to the edge of the crevasse that she had created, feeling the magic deep below. Something was coming—the same darkness that was at the base of my castle. *That* was expected. But there was something different about it. I frowned.

"What's happening?" a woman shouted behind me.

I spun back and saw the golden-haired woman. Carrow.

Another voice echoed, deep in my soul. *It is time, Hades.*

A chill of knowledge raced over me, confirming what I had already suspected.

The voice from my abyss, from the Place of Memories—it *was* Chronos. It always had been.

For millennia, I'd known my fate. Known exactly what I would do.

And everything was changing. In an instant, I knew that nothing was going to play out the way I'd expected it. The darkness was more than just an ephemeral force. It was a *Titan*.

I drew my bident from the ether, ready to fight. I would allow the darkness to spread—it had been my plan all along—but I would drive Chronos back into Tartarus. There was room for only ruler, and it would be me.

I turned back to Seraphia, seeing her sway on her

knees, leaning toward the crevasse. Chronos was rising, and she was giving up her life to trap him by healing the earth that she had damaged while trying to save her friends. But it would take everything inside of her. If she fell into that crevasse, she wouldn't die.

She'd end up in Tartarus.

No.

Whatever happened, I couldn't let her be trapped in that realm of torture.

The voice came again. *It is time for your choice, Hades. Time to join me.*

This was what Chronos had spoken of at the Place of Memories. Spreading the darkness also gave him a way to escape Tartarus. All these years, he had hidden it from me. Once, I would not have cared. I did only what I was commanded to do, a machine of death. I would have joined him.

No longer.

Instinct drove me as I plunged my hand into my pocket and withdrew the potion that her friend had made for her. It would allow her to leave the underworld if I blessed it. If I didn't survive this, I didn't want Seraphia trapped.

I gripped the potion tight and said, "I give Seraphia permission to leave the underworld with no ill effects."

In my hand, the bottle glowed warmly. It had worked. I shoved it at Carrow. "Give this to her."

Carrow frowned and took it.

I spun back to Seraphia, calling upon my wings. I needed to stop her before she lost consciousness and fell into the pit leading to Tartarus. But before I could launch myself into the air, Seraphia swayed, her eyes fluttering shut. In one horrifying second, she fell into the abyss and disappeared. At the same time, a dark shadow burst from the crack in the earth.

Chronos.

He landed on the ground next to the crevasse, ten feet tall and formed entirely of mist that solidified more with every second. Magic rolled out from him, so strong it shook my bones. His voice boomed as he spoke. "Join me, Hades."

"Never."

When I'd realized he might be trying to escape, I'd planned to force him back into Tartarus. But I couldn't do that *and* save Seraphia. There wasn't enough time. I had to choose.

Seraphia.

There was no question. I ignored Chronos and launched myself toward the crevasse, flying as fast as I could.

"If you do not join me, this is war."

Of course it was war. I did not care. His voice followed me down as the wind tore past me. "This will cement your curse, dooming you to eternity in Tartarus. Dooming *her*."

The hell it would. I flew faster, spotting her plummeting below me.

"Join me!" the voice bellowed, shaking the crevasse walls and causing dirt and rocks to tumble.

Never.

I didn't rule at the side of another. And I would never sacrifice Seraphia for such a thing.

My heart thundered as I flew, gaining on her. Gaining. I needed to get her before she reached Tartarus, or we would both be doomed. Panic made my heart thunder.

Finally, I reached her, plucking her from the air and yanking her to me, my soul calming as soon as I felt her in my arms. Gripping her tightly, I shot upward, racing toward the surface.

I clutched Seraphia with one arm as I drew my bident with the other. If Chronos awaited, it would be war. I'd made my choice, and it pitted me against the force that had made me. Wind tore past us as we rose, and I looked at Seraphia, fear rising as I saw her so still and pale.

Finally, I burst free to the surface.

The moonlight was so bright, it looked like daylight. It glittered on the water around the island, spreading a glow on the partially dead land that surrounded the crevasse.

Chronos was nowhere to be seen. He had disappeared. Escaped.

Carrow stared up at us, her eyes wide.

I flew away from her, not wanting to be near anyone else, and carried Seraphia to a rocky beach. I landed, going immediately to my knees as I cradled her against me.

"Wake, Seraphia."

She lay still and pale in my arms, her beautiful dark hair gleaming under the moonlight.

I pressed my hand to her chest and used my magic to heal her, drawing the death from her body. She was only partially gone, thank fates, but the seconds it took to heal her lasted a lifetime.

She gasped and opened her eyes, looking up at me. "Hades?"

"Seraphia." I pulled her to me, kissing her.

For the briefest moment, she kissed me back. Light exploded within me, glorious and bright, before I forced it away. Then she withdrew, her eyes wide. "What happened?"

Panting, I stared at her. All I wanted was to disappear into her embrace. But so much had happened.

What had I just done?

Conflict roared within me, the darkness and light at battle. Which would it be?

She pulled out of my arms and staggered upright, stepping away from me. "What happened?"

"You nearly fell into Tartarus." My tone was harsh, the fear of the memory driving me. I rose, facing her. I drew in a ragged breath, clinging to the dark that I had known for so long.

She nodded, understanding lighting her face. "I remember. I had to stop Chronos from rising. Did I?"

I shook my head. "No. He has escaped."

"What!" Horror stretched across her face. "You should have let me finish! It would have stopped him."

"Would it?" I asked the question, though I didn't care about the answer. Even if it would have stopped him, I'd never have let her sacrifice herself.

"Yes!" Anger flashed on her face. "This is all my fault."

"There is no fault if it is fate."

"So you're saying it's a good thing he's out?" She spun around, searching the land around us. Some of the grass was dead, and a few of the bushes. "Was this what you intended all along?"

"No. This is a complication."

"A *complication*? He's the personification of evil, and now he has escaped Tartarus."

"And I will deal with him. I will stop him. But I want you at my side."

She swallowed hard, her eyes huge. "At your side?"

"As my queen."

"And you're going to stop this terrible plan to spread the underworld to earth?"

"No, of course not." The idea was absurd. I'd sought this for millennia. It was all I knew. "I am going to stop

Chronos and take my place as the ruler of all. With you at my side." I held out my hand, remembering how she'd saved me. It was only because of her that I was even standing here. Desperation made my heart thunder. *Take my hand.* "Join me, Seraphia. Please."

She shook her head, eyes horrified. "I can't do that, Hades." She backed up farther, her hand outstretched as if to ward me off. "I thought you were changing. I thought you *had* changed. You could have fulfilled your goals here tonight. But instead, you saved me."

"I would never let anything happen to you. It doesn't mean I've given up my goal. Just delayed it."

"That's the problem."

Her voice was so stark, so set, that dread opened up inside me. She had appeared to turn to the dark, but she clearly hadn't. Would she not join me? "It is who I am. What I was made for. Be my queen, at my side."

A tear rolled down her pale cheek. "No."

She plunged a hand into her pocket and pulled something out. In the flash of an eye, she'd thrown it to the ground, stepped into the glittery gray cloud, and disappeared.

I stared at the space where she had been, devastated.

23

SERAPHIA

The ether flung me through space, spitting me out in the Haunted Hound a few moments later. I spun in a circle and spotted all of my friends standing near the bar. All except for Carrow.

As if she'd heard me, she appeared at my side, clearly having used a transport charm. "Are you all right?" she demanded. "I saw Hades save you."

"I'm fine." My heart felt like it had torn in two and I would never catch my breath, but at least I was here.

She hugged me tight. "Oh, thank fates. I couldn't believe it when I saw him jump into that pit after you."

I nodded and pulled back, head spinning. Desperate

to check on my friends, I turned toward Beatrix, Eve, and Mac. They looked whole and healthy, thank fates. I hurried to them, hugging each in turn.

Carrow joined us. "What just happened?"

I collapsed onto a bar stool. "So much."

"But you saved us," Mac said. "Again."

"I did so much worse." I swallowed hard. The words spilled out of my mouth, and I told them everything. Me, Hades, releasing Chronos.

"So, you're saying he's out there now?" said Mac.

"Yes." I nodded. "We had no idea, but it was his goal all along. Now he's free, and whatever he does, it's going to be terrible."

Eve nodded, her eyes shadowed. "The gods locked them up for a reason."

"And Hades wants to defeat Chronos and take control for himself?" Mac asked. "He still wants to spread the realm of the underworld to the earth?"

I nodded. "I've unleashed something. Started whatever it was that Hades wanted. Death will spread, and he's determined to rule it all."

"But he must care for you." Carrow reached into her pocket and withdrew the vial of potion that Eve had made. "He blessed this and gave it to me. He wanted you to have your freedom."

Shocked, I stared at the potion, then at her. "What? Why?"

She shrugged. "Maybe he thought he wouldn't survive. The figure of Chronos was telling him that he had to choose between power and you. That if he chose wrong, it would be war. He chose you."

My hand shook as it closed over the vial. He'd thought of everything. Blessing the potion had been a selfless act. I swallowed hard, reminding myself of our fight. "But now that he's saved me, he wants to have his cake and eat it, too."

"You and the power," Beatrix said. "He's hooked on you."

"He's hooked on the idea of power. He wants everything." *It's what he was created to want.*

I'd felt him turning to the light, but he'd still chosen the darkness.

As for me, in the end, I'd chosen the light. Too late, but I'd done it. I'd fought off the darkness and would have succeeded in stopping Chronos if Hades had let me continue. I was sure of it.

He could do the same.

Maybe it was foolish of me to keep trying, but I wanted so badly to believe that I could still save him.

"Take the potion, Seraphia." Carrow's no-nonsense voice broke through my thoughts. It was her guild leader voice, and it worked.

I uncorked the potion and gulped it down. As I swallowed, warmth spread through me. The physical discomfort that I felt from being out of the underworld disappeared, and I sighed, relieved. "It worked."

Carrow grinned and hugged me tight. "Thank fates that's over."

"Just that little bit is over." My mind whirled with all that was to come. "Hades can walk the earth now. I gave him that—it was part of the prophecy that once we spread the darkness to the earth, he could walk upon it. And Chronos is out."

"We have to stop Chronos," Mac said. "We've got to send him back."

I nodded, trying to contemplate how much damage he could do now that he was out. He was the darkness that had created Hades, the evilest part of humanity. And now he was free.

Hades was free.

"You're not giving up on Hades, are you?" Carrow asked.

I shook my head, knowing that it would be the smart thing. I didn't care. "I'm not."

I'd seen the goodness in him, the humanity. It was still growing. He'd saved me, after all. Given up his goal to protect me...well, at least in the short term.

"Where is he now?" Mac asked.

"I left him in Cyprus. But he's a god, so I'm sure he can get himself out of there." Where he would go, though, I had no idea. Would he come to me?

I wanted him to.

No matter how angry I was, or frightened, I still wanted it. I still wanted him.

~~~

Thank you for reading! Book three will be here in December.

ACKNOWLEDGMENTS

Thank you, Ben, for everything. There would be no books without you.

Thank you to CN Crawford for collaborating with me on this Hades project. It was so much fun to work with you on this and your input made the book so much better. For anyone reading, CN Crawford also has a Hades book out—*The Fallen.* Click here to get it.

Thank you to Jena O'Connor and Ash Fitzsimmons for your excellent editing. The book is immensely better because of you!

Thank you to Carlos Quevedo for the beautiful cover art and Orina Kafe for the amazing typography.

Thank you to Tom McIntosh of my FireSouls Facebook group for suggesting the name Echo for the bat. It was voted the best name!

AUTHOR'S NOTE

Hey there! I hope you enjoyed *Awakened*. I loved writing this book. Most of my books draw some inspiration from myth or history, and the Greek myth inspiration for *Awakened* was probably pretty obvious. My take on Hades involves wings he never had in the myth, and I'm playing pretty fast and loose with Chronos and the creation of Hades, but I stick fairly close to the use of pomegranate to draw Persephone back into the underworld.

I also drew inspiration from the oracle at Kamarina. There was a famous oracle at the ancient city, located in Sicily, who lived during the 5th century. However, I borrowed only the name. The true story involves a town besieged by plague. They asked their oracle if they should drain the swamp that surrounded the town in order to eliminate the plague. She said that they should not and should wait for it to pass. They didn't listen. Unfortunately, the swamp was the only thing protecting them from their enemies, the Carthaginians. Once it was drained, the Carthaginians marched into Kamarina and killed them all.

That's it for the history and myth in this book. Thank you for reading, and I hope you stick around with Hades and Persephone for the rest of their adventure!

ABOUT LINSEY

Before becoming a writer, Linsey Hall was a nautical archaeologist who studied shipwrecks from Hawaii and the Yukon to the UK and the Mediterranean. She credits fantasy and historical romances with her love of history and her career as an archaeologist. After a decade of tromping around the globe in search of old bits of stuff that people left lying about, she settled down and started penning her own romance novels. Her Dragon's Gift series draws upon her love of history and the paranormal elements that she can't help but include.

COPYRIGHT

Printed in Poland
by Amazon Fulfillment
Poland Sp. z o.o., Wrocław